T·H·E
FUTURE-TELLING LADY

A N D   O T H E R   S T O R I E S

J·A·M·E·S   B·E·R·R·Y

Willa Perlman Books

HarperTrophy
A Division of HarperCollins*Publishers*

To the memory of my mother

The Future-Telling Lady and Other Stories was first published in a slightly different form in England by Hamish Hamilton Ltd., under the title *The Future-Telling Lady*.

The Future-Telling Lady and Other Stories
Copyright © 1991 by James Berry
Manufactured in the United Kingdom by HarperCollins Publishers Ltd. For information address HarperCollins Children's Books, a division of HarperCollins Publishers, 10 East 53rd Street, New York, NY 10022.
The type is set in Lapidary and Lithos.
Typography by Anahid Hamparian

Library of Congress Cataloging-in-Publication Data
Berry, James
   The future telling lady, and other stories / James Berry.
      p.   cm.
   "Willa Perlman books."
   Contents: Cotton-tree ghosts—Magic to make you invisible—Banana-day trip—Son-Son fetches the mule—The future-telling lady—Mr. Mongoose and Mrs. Hen.
   ISBN 0-06-021434-1. — ISBN 0-06-021435-X (lib. bdg.)
   ISBN 0-06-440471-4 (pbk.)
   1. Children's stories, West Indian (English)   [1. West Indies—Fiction.   2. Short stories.]   I. Title
PZ7.B461735Fu   1993   92-13759
[Fic]—dc20   CIP
                                                                          AC

First Harper Trophy edition, 1995.

CONTENTS

COTTON-TREE GHOSTS

It was Sunday. It was a very bright, glassy, sun-hot day in Flametree Village. The village was settled along the edge of one big cattle-rearing estate. Long ago, all this piece of Jamaica was Arawak Indians' land. Then white landowners, Afro-Caribbean people, and a few Asian people lived in the settlement that became Flametree Village.

Today most people had gone to church. Those at home lounged about quietly on verandas or under backyard trees, reading the Bible or just snoozing. No wonder Flametree Village was having its special Sunday-quiet. The feeling of mystery in the day had a wide

1

loneliness you couldn't escape—that amazing Sunday-atmosphere! But out of it all, out of this day so imbued with holiness, something else, something most unexpected, happened.

Sherena Bignal was on the front veranda, writing up her schoolwork. She looked up, looked around, stood up. And leaving her exercise book with her pen in it and her note pages opened, Sherena moved quietly, tiptoeing about. She saw her father sleeping with the Bible beside him in the cool of the creeper-grown back veranda. She saw her mother stretched out asleep on her bed, under the gently moving curtains at the window.

Sherena left the house like a quiet flutter of breeze. She carried her empty red-patterned raffia bag over her shoulder. In her thin white dress, floppy blue hat, and blue canvas shoes, she was noticeable. But nobody was about to see her. She simply walked on nippily, and her neat and slender feet took her quickly in the quiet and hot sunny day. A short way along, Sherena turned off the village road. She was amazed that there wasn't a single other human movement or sound anywhere. And she loved it. She opened the gate, closed it, and came into the big cattle pasture.

On Friday the pasture was emptied of its cattle, which had been taken elsewhere. Sherena's excitement bounced up a bit more; she'd seen an almond tree. But she ignored this one. The tree was small and unreliable. She remembered that this year the tree had no almonds at all.

Her craving for almonds sharpened. Soon she'd collect her bagful! Take them back, break them open, and have a feast, eating them with coconut. Then drink a cool, cool glass of lemonade. Oh, what joy! Made your mouth water just thinking of it! Good thing she knew exactly where those two fabulous almond trees were. All loaded with green almonds hanging. With dropped ripe nuts all scattered around!

Sherena came to the sharp and gritty slope. Unexpectedly, she saw what seemed part of old ruins. Then she noticed what could have been an old entrance. She stepped closer. Almost hidden, covered with vines, under a tree branch, it could be the ruins of an ancient gateway pillar. Sherena was surprised. It seemed so mysterious! How's it she'd never seen it before? And not even known it existed? And the numberless times she'd been here— and passed here! Then, thinking of her almonds, the pillar went out of her head. She stepped off again, knowing that the gritty slope led up to a surprising flat of grassland. And best of all, her two enormously towering and spreading almond trees were there. And some flame trees were there too, spreading themselves even wider than the almond trees. Then, standing quite apart, there was the fantastic, thick, and wide-based Cotton-Tree. Its vast trunk tapered up and up majestically, as if it wanted its top to touch the sky.

She came up to the top of the slope, with all her thoughts concentrated purely on collecting her bagful of almond nuts. Sherena knew the land very well. Her head down, she walked on hurriedly, thinking of exactly what she was going to do. Then, with a smile on her face, Sherena looked up to greet her fabulous almond trees. The smile disappeared from her face. Her almond trees weren't there! Weren't there! The flame trees weren't there! Sherena looked around and around. She saw a big old house with gardens and old-fashioned white people. "The whole place is different!" she whispered. "What's happened? Jesu! Am I lost? The place is somewhere else. I'm at a strange people's place. Hope they don't have bad dogs. Hope I don't get in trouble. Where, where am I?" It flashed through Sherena's head she must be dreaming. But she couldn't remember lying down anywhere to go to sleep. She was glad nobody seemed to see her. She stood looking at the old-fashioned white gentlemen and white ladies, eating. Picnicking under the great Cotton-Tree! She watched. The people ate, drank, joked, and laughed. It was all very strange. Almost with a shock, she noticed the children—all white children—playing about. Mostly girls—in long, old-fashioned clothes with lots of ribbons. Some of them rolled hoops along and ran behind them, striking the hoops with a stick to keep them going. Other children played with a cup and a ball attached. The ball was tossed up and caught in the cup. Totally engrossed, Sherena stood watching, knowing she didn't want to be seen. She didn't know how she'd get away.

From nowhere, an older girl stood in front of her. And the strange, freckle-faced girl, with long, untidy blond hair, stretched her hand out to her. As they clasped hands, the girl said, "How do you do?"

"I'm well," Sherena answered.

"I know you are," the strange girl said.

Amazed, Sherena said, "You know me?"

"I know who you are."

Sherena stared into the freckled face and slowly shook her head. "No. No. I dohn know you at all. From when and where you got to know me?"

"Ah! I'll inform you of the connection. You

are the descendant of your father's great-grandfather's father and his grandfather, who was William, our coachman."

"William?"

"Yes, William. He brought us here every end-of-week. You see, still we love it here."

"Children!" somebody called. "Children! Come on!"

"That's Mother. I must go. My name is Magdalen. Good-bye."

Sherena looked. All the people had moved. And everything cleared up! In a flash, there was nobody! She looked around. She barely caught a glimpse of a carriage vanishing through the old gateway. She stood stunned. All was like the puzzle of a dream.

An almond fell from the tree and fell at her feet. Dreamily she looked at the browny-yellow husk of the nut, shaped like a small egg. She looked up again. Everything had come back to normal! She saw every tree, every thing, was there, in place, as she knew the land.

A terror whipped around Sherena and gripped her. She nearly fainted. She saved herself with her dread, her terrible horror, of being alone. Instead of fainting, she hit the Sunday quiet, cutting through the day with "Mamma!" And Sherena ran. She found herself running like crazy. She ran on and on, calling "Mamma!" as if a monster chased her.

When Sherena's mom heard the alarm in her voice, she was already in the yard. Breathless, she crashed into her mother's arms in the sitting room. "Wha's the matter? Wha's the matter?" Mrs. Bignal said. Her father rushed up, looking as anxious as her mother, who begged her, "Calm down, Shere. Calm down. Please."

Sherena thrashed about. "Mamma, I saw ghosts! I saw ghosts!"

"Calm yourself, now. Calm yourself!"

"Shere? You seen ghosts?" Mr. Bignal said excitedly.

"Yes, Daddy. Yes!"

"Where? Where you seen ghosts?"

"At almond trees, where I go to get almonds."

"Tha's not almond tree. Tha's Cotton-Tree!
Around midday now—Sunday. Girl, you seen
Cotton-Tree Ghosts! Easy. They harmless."

"You feeling better?" her mother asked.

"Yes, Ma'am."

"Come. Si'down. Si'down, now."

"I'm still alive, Ma'am?"

The parents laughed. "Yes, sweetheart," her
mother said. "You still very much alive."

"Dohn laugh, Ma'am. Feel my hand. Feel it.
Is it ahright?"

"I feeling it. Is ahright."

"I'm alive, yes?"

"Of course you're alive."

"Ma'am, I shake hands with a ghost!"

"Huh-huh?" Mr. Bignal said. "You actually
shake hands with Magdalen?"

"Yeahs! You know about Magdalen, Dad?
She's known about?"

"Yes, Sherena. Magdalen is known about.
She always wahn to shake hands. And she

always leaves her name. She did, didn' she?"

"Yeahs!" Sherena sat up crossly. "Then how's it I knew nothing? Nothing—about Cotton-Tree Ghosts? Nobody ever said a word!"

"Children dohn know those things these days," her mother said. "It's—it's a long long time since anybody mentioned the ghosts."

"They always come at midday, then?"

"Yeh," said Mr. Bignal. "And on a Sunday. People who see them always see them around twelve a'clock—on Sunday, when all quiet. When the hot midday sunlight a-shimmer. And nobody about. And there's no human noise. Only bird-singing. And occasional animal cry. And the ghosts come. And bring all another world altogether! Fantastic!" Sherena's dad became thoughtful. Then he went on, "And, Shere—you saw—actually saw—the whole family?"

"Yeahs, Dad! The whole white family and friends! With children playing about. Incredible! Incredible! Is a dream you will never forget! And I knew nothing. Knew nothing about these incredible visitors!"

"They harmless, sweetheart. Harmless. I tell you, I envy you. I never seen them. As a young fellow, I spent many Sundays at Cotton-Tree, waiting to see the white-people ghosts. And get a handshake from Magdalen. But nothing! Jus' cahn see them."

"Magdalen told me she knew who I was."

"Huh-huh!" her dad said. "Did she?"

"She said she could inform me of my connection."

"Huh-huh! Did she?" her dad said. "Go on then."

"She said—wait, I must remember this—said, 'You are the descendant of your father's great-grandfather's father and his grandfather, who was William, our coachman.'"

"Fantastic."

"Dad, did you know about a coachman William—going way back?"

"No. Not at all. Not at all. But—I'll tell you—"

"Isn' there something," Mrs. Bignal said, "about the whole family drowning in the sea flood of the Port Royal earthquake?"

"Yes, yes. I was going to say that."

"That was the earthquake of 1692," Sherena said, "that destroyed our town of Port Royal?"

"Correct," Mr. Bignal said, "correct. The story goes that the ol' man of the ghost family used to be wealthy. It goes that he was a merchant and a law man at Port Royal. And along with his town house, he owned the land here with its big country house."

"Yes, yes!" Sherena said. "Magdalen said William used to drive them in their carriage to their country house, at the end-of-week."

"Fascinating. Also," Mr. Bignal said, "the story goes that the whole family died having lunch. Drowned suddenly, in the crazy ringing of the church bells, as the earthquake broke up the churches. And the bells all ringing their own ring till the sea swallowed them."

"What did the ghost women look like?"

Mrs. Bignal asked.

"Old-fashioned," Sherena said. "All old-fashioned. All puffed sleeves, long, blown-out dresses. And ribbons, ribbons, ribbons!"

"And the men?"

"Straight, oily-looking long hair, parted in the middle. And handlebar moustaches with a pointed twist at the end."

"Shere, sweetheart," Mr. Bignal said, "how did it actually feel, shaking hands with a ghost?"

Sherena shivered. "Dad, Dad, dohn remind me. Dohn remind me, please, please! Is too horrible now." She looked at her hand. "Hand, you held a ghost. You ahright? You not turned white or shriveled up or something?"

Her dad insisted, "Sweetheart, when there holding on to Magdalen's hand, did it feel like air, or an ordinary hand, or what?"

"Oh, Dad! It was all ordinary. Like meeting any stranger. The awful awful horrors come on afterward. Like now."

"Her voice—how did that sound?"

"Her voice?"

"Yes."

"When it was happening I expected it the way it sounded. Now——I imagine, her voice, like very, very ancient royal-family voice. Ever so, ever so loaded. With everything extra."

"Bet you, Sherena," her mother said, "you not going to pick up almonds when you dohn go to church?"

"Me, Mom? Oh, Lord have mercy! Never! Not on a Sunday. Not anytime at Cotton-Tree. Me one not ever going to that place again!"

"Dohn worry," her dad said. "Is all harmless if you dohn worry."

"Why?" Sherena asked. "Dad, why d'you think the ghosts leave from wherever they are to come back here?"

"Dohn know, Shere, sweetheart. Maybe—— they attached to the place. They like to come back. Maybe——because once the white people belong to here——they always part of it. Who knows?"

MAGIC TO MAKE YOU INVISIBLE

That Julian had too much time for himself!
She had too little time for herself, to do what
she liked. Now—Saturday morning—she was
left to clean the house. Nothing about this was
fair.

Yuumi dusted and tidied up, feeling really
cross. Puppa was gone to help another man
with some work. Mumma, as usual, took vegetables, fruits, and eggs to the town market to
sell. And what about her younger brother, Julian? Wasn't the Mr. Julian gone sea swimming? With friends? Just as he did every

Saturday morning? So, alone, she was house cleaning. Isn't it great, how something like a miracle has happened, that will change everything. Everything!

Every time—well, nearly every time—Puppa talked to Julian, Puppa put his arm around him. Nearly every time Puppa came home, out from his pocket came sweets, or something, for who? For Julian. Mumma did about the same thing, adding a kiss. They hardly remember she was there. Hardly they even think of her, the girl Yuuni, the older one, twelve years old. Her parents took no notice of that. In the same way they took no notice Julian was her most hurtful problem. Now they'll know nothing that she'd found a way to deal with her problem.

Yuuni stopped cleaning the mirror. She stopped as she remembered she'd woken up this morning with the most fantastic dream in her head. She'd rushed to the Bible. She'd opened the Bible and rustled through the thin leaves quick, quick. And there it was. The exact verse from her dream was correct. It was right. She knew now everything, everything else, would work. Funny how everybody always said she was like her father. And she was really turning out to be a miracle dreamer like him. Full of thinking, Yuuni sat down.

Only weeks ago, her puppa's dream won him fifty thousand dollars. He'd dreamed the number of the lottery ticket. Seen the exact number in his dream! And it won top prize— all that mighty lot of money. Now she herself had dreamed something mighty big. She'd dreamed how to make Julian invisible. Yuuni giggled: Julian totally invisible! And she remembered everything in the dream. Everything! Thinking of the magic, Yuuni actually gave a shiver. Her slim body shook. Her heartbeat went faster. The strange magic feeling scared her. But the peculiar feeling also gave her exciting sensations. "Julian totally invisible" echoed in her head. She giggled again, got up, and went on with her work.

Julian came home happily on his bicycle.

He came whistling into the open, airy, and sun-lit little bungalow. Yuuni heard and saw him. Then she heard him searching the kitchen and dining room but stayed quiet, thinking, "Listen to that bossy greedy guts! As usual turning the place upside down for food after enjoying himself!"

Julian came out on the veranda, eating. He carried thick pieces of bun and cheese on a plate, and a mug of iced lemonade he'd mixed. Changed into his white shirt with the lion head printed on the chest, he put everything on the little table, sat down, and went on eating. Yuuni came out too, barefoot, carrying a glass of lemonade. Her string-waisted skirt and short blouse left Yuuni's midriff bare. She leaned forward and said, "Something fantastic happened, Julian!"

Julian looked up. "Yeh?" Mixed cheese, bun, and lemonade filled his mouth.

"You know Puppa's dream won him that pile of money?"

"Yes, yeh."

"And it made his picture get in the news-papers?"

"Yeh."

"And it made him buy us new things, though mostly for you—with a new room be-ing built on the house for you and all."

"Well, well—okay. Okay."

"And people, even strangers, come to the house smiling at him, hoping to get a dollar or two? And some do?"

"Yes."

"Well—last night—I myself had a dream. A magic dream."

Julian was excited. "You dream a lottery number, too!"

"No. Something else."

"What? What, Yuuni?"

"I dream how to make somebody invisi-ble."

Julian went dumb for some seconds. Then pieces of hot potatoes seemed to come into his mouth when he tried to speak. "In-vi-vi-vi-visible? Can't be seen?"

Yuuni nodded. "Yes. That's it. Have it in my head right now."

"Right now you have that trick in you?"

"How to make somebody transparent? Totally transparent? So no eyes can see him? All here in my head."

"But Yuuni—tha's magic! Tha's bigger—much bigger—than Puppa's fifty thousand dollars. You're mightier, a mightier dreamer than Puppa."

"It gets me like that too."

Julian popped his eyes. "What you going to do with it?"

Yuuni was cool. "I'm talking to you. Nobody else."

Julian got up and walked a half circle. "Yuuni—Sista Yuuni—we could work wonders!"

"Like what?"

Julian clenched his fists and held them tight. "Yuuni, this is fantasplosive." He used one of his made-up big words that his friends used back to him. *Fantasplosive,*" he repeated. And more of his own language followed. "This is real sensation dizzy-dizzy. You going tell anybody?"

"You think I'm stupid? I'm only telling you."

"Wow, wow, whoopee! What a whoopee!"

"You'll have to help me to make it work, Julian."

"Help you? I'm your partner. Let's make it work now. Let's try it out. Try it out right away."

"Not yet. Not yet. You can only see how it works as we go along."

"Okay, then. Okay."

"What would you like to do with this magic, yourself?"

"Wow! No end to it, Yuuni."

"What, for example?"

"Well—first of all—you know that boy Lester Davis?"

"Yeh."

"Lester Davis is always tripping me up and go on all sorry like. It'd be fantasplosion keeping on tripping him up. And he can see no-

21

body. Nobody who's doing it. Then all those sudden backslappers. Boy, wouldn't I surprise them. They're having a serious conversation and *whack!* and *whack!* in the middle of the back. Wow! Then, then, with this magic, I can pick my lessons. Those I hate, I just show up to be seen. Then I'm not there."

"Anything else?"

"Just once—one time only—it'd be a wow to shove Lester Davis in front of the headmaster as he's passing us kids, to see the two tangled up on the ground together." Julian laughed with enjoyment. Yuuni couldn't help laughing too. "But, the best, best joke," Julian went on, "would be picking cakes off the cake-seller tray at school yard. Just to see her face, as one by one every cake disappears from her tray." Julian laughed. "Fantasplosion! She'd die, wouldn't she? They'd have to get out the first-aid kit."

"What about house cleaning, dish washing, food preparing for cooking, and all that?"

"Yes, yeh. You yourself could baffle

Mumma. Couldn't you? And same way with me. When they want me do a job, I just disappear. I'm nowhere. Though was just there. Just there! They call; I'm nowhere." Excitement in his eyes, Julian grinned. "Sensation, oh sensation! Yuuni, come on. Let's start up the magic. Mumma and Puppa not here till later. It's a good time."

"I can't tell you anything before we're doing it. Understand? So don't ask, don't insist, don't do anything to spoil anything. Right?"

Julian raised his opened hands to Yuuni, in submission and agreement, and said, "I swear. I swear to be obedient."

"Right. I can tell you a little bit now. Monday's a school holiday. That'll make everything perfect. We need today, tomorrow, and Monday. That is, from today to twelve o'clock on the third day. We have to be careful to turn things magical on the third day. We must."

"Okay. I know three is a magic number. I know that."

"You know that?"

"Yeh."

"Jesus died at the age of thirty-three at three o'clock. Did you know that?"

"No. I didn't know that."

"There you are. You don't know everything."

"My leader, I follow. I'm jobless for a job."

"You'll have to catch three dragonflies."

"Three needlepoints? As part of the magic?"

"As part of the preparation."

"Oh, boy! Big job. Any questions allowed?"

"No questions allowed."

"Well—I'll have to get some gum."

"Will take too long to tap a tree for gum."

"I think—I think I could get some gum from Benji."

"Then, go and get the gum from Benji."

Julian wheeled away on his bicycle. It didn't take him long to come back with some tacky gum in a piece of coconut shell. "I'll go and set the gum for the needlepoints," he told Yuuni.

"Okay. Set the gum, leave it and come back."

Again Julian wheeled away off on his bicycle. At the pond in the pasture, swarms of dragonflies and butterflies flew over and around the pool of water, and were also perched on the dry tops of stems and other water plants. Bare twiggy tops of stems were places to set the gum. Julian set his gum traps and came back home.

"I'm ready for our next job," Yuuni said. "See I've got my shoes on."

"Information needed," Julian said. "What's this job?"

"Getting three ratbats."

"Ratbats?"

"Yes."

"They're ugly, awful, disgusting creatures! And live in a cave."

"All true. But must get three of them."

"You'll have to do the catching and the holding them," Julian said.

"Ahright," Yuuni said. "I'll do the catching.

25

I'll hold them. And we've got to be quick. We got to get back before Mumma or Puppa gets home."

"Bottomwood Caves not too far."

"That's right. We go there."

Yunni and Julian walked across the cow pasture. They came along and heard the sea. Then they climbed the leafy, creeper-covered rocky hillside facing the sea. Yuuni leading the way, they turned into a cave entrance and went on in.

Julian turned on the flashlight and moved the shining light about. The dark, stinking underground space went on all around. Bats hung head downward, asleep, singly or in clusters. Julian thought this must have been a burial place for some Arawak Indians long, long time ago. As he and his sister moved on into the dark, smelly, and scary cave, their feet kept sinking into ages of bat droppings.

"Beginning of hell this," Julian whispered. "Creepy as worms."

"Horrible," Yuuni whispered back. "But

we won't be long."

Julian stopped. "I go no further. Snakes, scorpions, everything, must be here. Satan himself could suddenly collar you here."

"There, look! Some together just overhead here."

A couple of steps and light held closely on the sleeping brown bats made them give a little dozy shiver. A towel in her hand, the determined Yuuni grabbed a bunch of the hanging bats and stuffed them in the white pillowcase she carried. Outside the cave, they checked. Yuuni had grabbed exactly three bats. Going home, Yuuni and Julian stopped at the pond and also collected up exactly three trapped dragonflies.

At home, Yunni smiled to herself. Everything has worked well. Totally well! Full success with everything is a good, good sign. But more things to be done.

Yunni sent Julian off again. He came back with three white wing feathers from a village man's white pigeon. And now it was time to get everything together that made the magic.

Yuuni tied up the three bats in one white handkerchief and the three dragonflies in another. She put three cups of water in a saucepan, and then put in the encased bats and dragonflies. She covered the saucepan and let it boil three quarters of an hour. Keeping strict time, Yuuni poured off the magic liquid stock from the saucepan into a jug and put it in a safe place to cool. She then made Julian bury the cooked bats and dragonflies with a little wooden cross over them.

The magic stock cooled, and Yuuni put it into a drinking glass. Out of her pocket, she took a page torn from the Bible; it was the whole page of Psalm 3. She folded the Bible page into three and carefully let it stand in the magic stock in the glass. She put the drinking glass with everything in a bigger jar, and put the three white feathers to stand outside the glass in the jar. She placed a wooden cross on top of the glass and carefully fitted on the lid of the jar. Finally, taking great care, Yuuni and

Julian buried the jar and marked the spot with a heavy stone.

To have to wait till the third day for the working of the magic was the hardest test for Yuuni and Julian. Though excited and impatient Julian slept well. Twice, Yuuni woke up and giggled at the thought of turning Julian invisible. It unexpectedly struck Yuuni that, when Julian became invisible, she wouldn't know how to make him real again. That wasn't in the dream. Well——she'd have to take a chance on that. Something would make him come back real, at some time. As long as she could make him invisible when she liked, that was what mattered.

On the second day, in the evening, Julian whispered to Yuuni, "The stone's still there in place."

She answered quietly. "I know."

Twelve o'clock Monday, at the end of the backyard, Yuuni and Julian dug up their secret magic jar. Yuuni held the glass with the cross on it. She looked unblinking into Julian's eyes and said, "At my command, when this drink is drunk and has disappeared, Julian, you will be unseeable." She removed the cross from the top of the glass, stepped forward, and made the sign of the cross on Julian's forehead. She handed him the glass and said, "Drink this drink, Julian."

Julian took the magic drink. He lifted the glass and swallowed down the cold and nasty brothy soup and winced. He stood blinking hard, testing himself to see how he felt. Sensation dizzy-dizzy now! Was he normal? "Can you see me?" he asked.

"First time—I can't tell," Yuuni said. "We have to try it out on somebody else."

"Really?" Julian said, sounding and looking as if he didn't know whether he was really alive or not.

"Let's go and see if Mumma can see you."

Julian looked doubtful about what to do, but said, "Okay. I'll see if Mumma can see me."

"Go carefully like. Carefully," Yuuni said unnecessarily.

Julian walked up from the backyard, feeling and looking like a zombie. He went into the kitchen, trying to creep up quietly on his mother, who stood at the table preparing lunch. Half hiding, Yuuni stood in the doorway.

"What the devil you come creeping behind me about?" his mother said crossly. "What you playing at? Eh? I was looking for you, anyway. Take the bucket and get a couple of buckets of water. And where's that sister of yours? Eh? Where's she?"

Fantasplosion! The magic didn't work! After all that trouble! Yet all over himself Julian felt a great, great relief. The taste of the nasty magic soup was still in his mouth. He picked up the bucket. He went out to get water from the standing pipe at the roadside. Yuuni slunk into the kitchen, feeling really down with disappointment. She sighed sadly but began helping her mother.

Yet if Yuuni's mother had known what she and her brother had done to the helpless bats and dragonflies, Yuuni wouldn't only have sighed. Her mother would have made her cry. But who could tell? When the parents found the missing Bible leaf and all was revealed, who could say what might happen?

Julian took a long time coming back with the water. His mother was suddenly concerned. Right away Yuuni said she'd go and find him. She rushed out and ran up the road.

Nobody was at the roadside standing pipe, only Julian's bucket. Yuuni clasped her face in shock. "Julian!" she whispered nervously, looking all around. "Are you here?" She stretched out her arms, moving around and around, feeling the air, to see if Julian was there. "Julian?" She stood. "Julian? Are you here? Somewhere?"

No answer. Yuuni was frightened. Then she heard coughing. Someone was being sick. Where did the coughing come from? Yuuni listened carefully. The throwing-up coughing went again. Yuuni spun herself around. Where? Where did it come from? It could have come from anywhere, she thought. "It's happened," she whispered. "He's gone invisible! But the magic mixture is making him sick. . . . Perhaps he could die. Suppose he died?" Tears came quickly into Yuuni's eyes. She hugged herself tightly. "Oh God, my brother's bodyless! Dear God, Dear God, give him back a body to go with his voice. Do, give him back his body to go with his voice. Do . . ."

Yuuni looked and saw Julian climbing over the property wall he'd hidden behind. "Julian," she said, "you've tricked me!"

"I was being sick, and saw you coming. I was thinking Mumma would follow. So I jumped over the wall."

"So you're back!" Yuuni said. She turned and walked off crossly, thinking, He's back! We'll have to do it all over again. And make it work. Make it work.

BANANA-DAY TRIP

"Boy-Don, you're dressed up and ready!" Playfully teasing, big brother Andy stared at him. "You all ready to go to Granny!"

There on the front veranda, brushing down his dog, Boy-Don was cool. "Yes, I'm ready. And man, I kinda could like no problems from you. Telling me I'm too early. Or anything like that."

Acting all repentant, fourteen-year-old Andy put his hands together, as if he was praying, asking forgiveness. He shook his head. "No. No, Boy-Don! You want to be two hours early. I would *never* be the one to interfere one bit."

34

Boy-Don called out loudly. "Mamma? Mamma?"

"Yeahs!" his mom answered from a side room of the sprawling bungalow. Both Mrs. and Mr. Wallman were head teachers. Though it was school holidays, they were over papers at their desks in the house, working.

"Is it true, Mamma, I have to wait two hours?"

"Not true. Ignore your brother, Andy."

"You think, Mamma—per'aps—Mr. Burke forgot to call for me?"

"No, Boy-Don. Mr. Burke won't forget. Just be patient."

Boy-Don gave Andy one cross look and went on slowly brushing down his dog, Browndash. Before Andy could say anything else, their dad called him to go and do a job. Looking at his younger brother, Andy went with his face full of a teasing smile. What Andy didn't know was that as he turned his back, Boy-Don also had a glint of happy mischief in his eye. He knew Andy and Hannah were jealous of his trip alone to Granny. For him, Boy-Don, their jealousy made his going away bigger, more exciting, more special, more stupendous.

Dressed in his cleaned sneakers, his fresh blue-denim trousers, denim short-sleeved shirt, and denim long-fronted cap turned sideways on his head, Boy-Don brushed his dog. But he kept his ears cocked sharp. All the time he listened. He listened to pick out the distant horn blowing of Mr. Burke's loaded banana truck that would take him to Granny-May's house. He'd stay there one whole week!

From nowhere, twelve-year-old Hannah popped out onto the veranda. She sat down in a deck chair. Boy-Don said, "My sister—you come to keep me company or to trouble me?"

"Why you so impatient to get away?"

"I'm not on my way to Granny yet. Mr. Burke's taking ages getting me away from you."

"Boy-Don, I was thinking. I had to come and talk to you. D'you know exactly why *you* are going to stay with Granny-May and not me? Or Andy? Or Mark?"

Boy-Don tossed his arms about. "Jealous! Jealous! Jealous!"

"Favoritism! That's what it is. Favoritism!"

Boy-Don stood with Browndash and faced Hannah crossly. "Granny-May love me best. She love me best. Me is the one she love best."

"Listen to him! Listen to him! Can't even talk properly. If Mamma could hear you. Don't you know when to say, 'Granny-May *loves* me best?' Instead of 'love,' '*love* me best'? And haven't you learned yet how to say, 'I am the one she *loves* best'? Instead of 'me,' '*me* is the one'?"

Boy-Don frowned in a scared way, looking around. He didn't want their mom to hear at all. "Ahright! Ahright!" he said in a hushed voice. "Next time I say it properly. Next time. Next time."

"All that bad talk. Talking all that bad talk to Granny-May. See now why I'd be the fit person to go for the week? See now?"

"You know lots of things already. Lots of things what correct. I'll benefit. I'll learn something."

"There you go again. There you go with 'lots of things what correct.' You must say, 'lots of things *that are* correct.'"

"You could make me go wrong and go wrong and go wrong by telling me, telling me all the time I'm wrong."

"I'm trying to point out to you something all obvious. If I was the one going to Granny-May, I'd have a lot, lot more that's interesting to say there, and say when I get back. Understand that?"

Boy-Don turned to brushing his dog again. "You'll see if I don't have lots, lots that's interesting when I get back."

"We'll see. We will all see. I know. I get it."

"Get what?"

"Your big thing in mind is to do rap rhymes about Granny-May."

Boy-Don protested. "No! Granny-May is the best. I would never pull a joke on Granny-

38

May. Never! That's what I do to you. But never Granny-May."

"I should've asked Granny-May to let me come along to look after you. You know that?"

Offended like a teased dog, Boy-Don turned around swiftly and yapped. "You crazy? You mad? Who'd want you to come? You not dumb. You know when somebody is specially invited and when somebody else specially *not* invited."

"I had to pack your bag for you."

"And I had to stop you putting in schoolbooks and too much clothes."

"Going to wear your cap front sideways at Granny's?"

"My business, Hannah! My business!" He turned his back on her.

She leaped up. "Okay. If you're going to be rude, I'll just go."

"And great riddance."

"We'll see what you have to say that's of any interest whatsoever when you get back. We'll just wait and see!" And Hannah was gone.

There was kind of mock-cross affection between Hannah and Boy-Don. They argued a lot. Hannah would never admit how much Boy-Don's rap rhymes and performances amused her. She called his rap rhymes "silly forced-ripe verse." Yet she'd get at him, set him up to perform, making it look as if it was for their dad. The first time that Boy-Don excitedly got everybody together to hear his rap rhymes, Hannah whispered to herself, "Fantastic! Brilliant!" Wide-eyed, she'd been amazed he could do what he did. Hannah would never let on that, getting Boy-Don to do it for her over and over, she'd memorized every word. And standing in front of the mirror, she'd practiced and imitated his style. She only had to think of it, and close her eyes, and there was Boy-Don performing.

His cap front was turned sideways over one ear, head nodding, arms swinging in strict-rhythm dance. His poem came from memory—

"I'm the boy called Boy-Don,
well known as number-one style man,
with only that bother of a sister
and each of the other called brother.

"But I done them in with new craze.
I leave them in old-time days,
the way me one wear my cap
with my style rap.

"Everywhere people like to see me.
Everywhere people like to hear me,
this boy called Boy-Don
the number-one style man,
the number-one style man. . . ."

All as excited as he was about going away,
Boy-Don had not forgotten his jobs he had to
do. One by one he'd done what he could.
What he couldn't finish, he fixed up for somebody to do while he was away. These jobs were
to do with animals given to him by relatives.
His goat he called Goaty; his pig he called

Rhino; his dog, of course, he called Brown-dash. He gave each animal its own special care. He used to ride the pig and goat around the yard. When he was lying down on the ve-randa, drawing or writing his rap rhymes, Boy-Don would have Goaty, Rhino, and Browndash lying down on the floor around him.

His going away made him work for them. For some days he'd spent his time cutting grass, bringing it, and piling it up for Goaty to eat while he was away. Andy had promised to give Goaty some of the special grass daily—saying it was from Boy-Don. He'd also pre-pared special feed for Rhino. Again, Andy promised he'd feed the pig, telling it was from Boy-Don. Hannah had promised she'd give Browndash his special dog bits, saying Boy-Don had left them for him. Nobody had to bathe the dog. Boy-Don had done that himself yesterday.

Boy-Don called loudly, "Mamma? . . . Mamma? . . . Mamma?"

At last his mom answered, "Yeahs!"

"Mr. Burke isn't coming for me."

"Yeahs—he will. Just wait. And please don't bother me."

That reassurance cheered up Boy-Don. He sat down comfortably in a deck chair with his dog and travel bag beside him. He'd been thinking perhaps he really should have gone on either a mini bus or the big bus. *But* it was Mr. Burke's banana truck he'd begged his parents to let him go with. It was great how he lived near a banana plantation and near a banana packing house, how Mr. Burke was a neighbor, how he was a planter himself and owner-driver of a banana truck. And his great truck carried bananas to the wharf for ships that carried them overseas to different, different cities of the world! To think that bananas he knew and watched develop should travel to cities overseas pleased, thrilled, and fascinated him no end.

Hannah came back and pretended to be ever so surprised. "Oh, Mr. Big-Talk Traveler is still here!" The sound of Hannah's words became mixed with the horn blowing of a distant truck.

Boy-Don leaped up, shouting. "He's coming! He's coming! Mr. Burke's coming!" He dashed inside, kissed his mom, dashed to another room, kissed his dad, and was outside again, bag in hand. The big, long, loaded truck stopped in a fanfare of horn blowing at the gate. Its load was covered with a green tarpaulin. It kept its engine running while the whole family came out. Boy-Don climbed up, went in the cab and sat beside Mr. Burke. In its ear-splitting horn blowing, the truck drove off. Everybody waved good-bye. Boy-Don waved back, feeling great. At that moment he didn't mind at all if he never came back, ever.

Boy-Don's head moved from side to side, looking through the windshield of the truck and its open windows. The fields of coconut trees that they passed, like the grazing cattle pasture, looked all different from inside the cab of a loaded, moving banana truck.

The smiling-faced Mr. Burke was quite a talker. "Banana Day gets the fields and packinghouse lively and bustling. And the trucks on the road. Eh, Boy-Don?"

"Yes, sir. Some people get money."

"You know it, man. You know it."

"Yes."

"When I was your age, a banana market day was different."

"Different, sir?"

"Oh, yeh. Those days, whole village goes abustle with banana selling. Mostly everybody sells a bunch or two. Bananas come from mountain land, lowland, yard land—all about—on donkey, mule, horse, or carried by villager. Extra money comes to women to shop. Rum shops livelier with men. Everybody gets a little share. Now—requirements change. Competition fiercer. Better-quality fruit is demanded. Small-man grower sells locally. Only big planters can manage it fo' overseas market."

Boy-Don was surprised. He thought banana

growing had always been the same. His thinking flashed on how Mr. Burke's field of bananas near his home was given all kind of special, special care. Hanging bunches of bananas were fattened up in a green mesh sack, like a lady's glove up her arm full length. That kept the bunch free of insect or leaf scratch. He found he somehow had a funny sort of envy for the travel and faraway life of bananas. He imagined how the bananas would travel on a ship on that big, big sea, all landless, touching the skyline all around. And the bananas would arrive in a city like another world. Surrounded by a foreign language, they'd get carried in gold baskets. In a strange home they'd get arranged in a bowl all gold. And some would get cooked in frying pans with gold handles. He remembered how when his brother-and-sister cousins from New York visited, he took them to their land up the bush on a donkey. He took them coconut and mango picking and sea bathing. He took them to the banana packinghouse. But best of all was taking them jumping the irrigation ditches—playing a game of crisscrossing in the air—in Mr. Burke's banana field. . . . He said, "And so banana day different now, sir?"

"One thing not changed, Boy-Don."

"What's that?"

"Waiting at the wharf to get unloaded onto the ship."

"You have to wait while the ship's waiting?"

"Long line of trucks will be there before me, loading on."

The docked ship and the bananas being loaded on made Boy-Don think. He was glad Mr. Burke went quiet. Then he began watching how Mr. Burke drove the truck. Going around corners, he pressed the horn on and on like a machine giving money, making a great ten-trumpets fanfare noise. The mountain of a load made the engine moan uphill and, like a welcome relief, changed downhill to a sound all relaxed. Mr. Burke drove through villages blowing his horn, making pigs, goats, dogs, or fowl scuttle off out of the way for dear life.

When Mr. Burke rested longest on his full-blast ten-trumpets horn, they had stopped four miles from the town, at Granny-May's house. And there was Granny-May and Miss Gee hurrying down toward the closed white gate.

They were dressed differently, in their own neat homemade summer frocks. Miss Gee's dress had leaf patterns, while Granny-May's was plain white and she had a stack of thin, colored bracelets on her wrists. Though Miss Gee was older, the tall and slim sisters looked similar, smiling together as they came to the gate.

Looking down from her tall height, Granny-May said, "Nicholas! Boy! What a way you've got big, and beautiful! Let me hug you and kiss you." But while she hugged and kissed Boy-Don, he felt surprised, sad, and disappointed that Granny-May called him Nicholas. Nowadays nobody called him Nicholas. And Miss Gee went through all the hugging and kissing too, adding more. Boy-Don felt helpless and shocked at how everybody knew his new name except them.

The way his new name had come to him was like a real miracle. Clear-clear, it all came back in his head. . . .

That day at school—a really vile and vicious day! He'd come home fed up, looking terrible, nothing but misery. He knew he had the silliest, stupidest name in the whole world. His name was worries! Everywhere—in whispers in class, in shouts on the school playground, on the road going home—"Knickers!" "Knickers!" "Want a game, Knickers?" Or the stupid, "Hi there, Nick-the-Nicker-to-be-Nicked-for-Nicking!" "How's Nick-the-Nicker?" "Nick-the-Knickers, hi there!"

Oh, it was bad. Feeling all terrible and fed up, he'd sat on the back veranda. Hannah had come and sat on the bench. "I have the worst-worst name in the world," he'd said.

"What you mean?"

"I just mean I have the stupidest name."

"Nicholas is a great, brilliant name."

"Nicholas, Nick, Nickers—I hate it!"

"Wait. Wait here a minute." Hannah got

up, went, came back with the encyclopedia, and read from it. Hannah first explained that because his birthday was December sixth, their parents honored his birthday by naming him after Saint Nicholas. She read how Saint Nicholas's life was full of giving gifts and doing good deeds. And Saint Nicholas was so important that his saintly feast-day celebration was changed from December sixth, so that it could be kept up on Christmas Day.

"But nobody at school knows anything about all that!" he'd said crossly.

"That's because they're ignorant and stupid."

"Then why even you have to read it from a book? And not just tell me out of your head?"

"Because I want to show you it's true."

"Well, I don't believe it. And nobody at school would believe."

"Then you should explain how important your name is."

"Have you ever been laughed at by everybody? Eh? Have you ever been laughed at?"

"Of course I have."

"I have an idea." He'd said that quietly, holding his head down.

"What idea?" Hannah said doubtfully.

"You know our dad's name is Mr. Donald Wallman?"

"Of course I know that."

"So—he's a big-man Don."

"What you getting at?"

He'd jumped up and shouted. "Our dad's Big-Don! I am Boy-Don! Boy-Don's my real name. That's my name—Boy-Don!"

"Ahh! Stupid!" his sister had sneered. "And who, who's going to take the slightest bit of notice of any 'Boy-Don'?"

"I'm doing some rap rhymes to go with it."

"Some what?"

"Rap rhymes."

"What's that?"

"You know rapping! Anyway, you'll see. And I have something special to go with it. I have a special cap-wearing style to go with my rap rhymes. . . ."

And, boy, the whole thing worked like the magic of iced lemonade! Everybody wanted it.

All the girls and boys wanted him over and over to perform his rap rhymes. Everybody wanted to see his style of dance with his rap sound going—

"I'm the boy called Boy-Don,
well known as number-one style man . . .
the way me one wear my cap
with my style of rap . . ."

It went on in the school playground. On the school road it went on. "Boy-Don! Boy-Don!" the girls and boys shouted. "Perform 'Boy Called Boy-Don'!" "Perform 'Boy-Don'!" "Do 'Mighty Frog'!" "Yes, do 'Mighty-Frog'!" "No, no. Do 'Long Face, Hee-haw'!" They shouted, "Do it again! Again! Again!" Twice, up at village square, Saturday evenings, he did "Mighty Frog" over and over. Cap turned sideways, arms swinging in rhythm, head nodding—

"In the lane at my trot of a jog,
I met the one Mighty Frog.
I looked him up,
he looked me up.
I looked him down,
he looked me down.
Then I said, 'Hello, bush folk.'
      Then he said 'GROAK, GROAK.'

"I jumped around. 'Hello, bush folk.'
He jumped around, 'GROAK, GROAK.
   GROAK, GROAK.'
We danced in bright moonlight,
danced around on till daylight.
Boy-Don—'Hello, bush folk,'
Mighty Frog—'GROAK, GROAK.
   GROAK, GROAK.'

"Mighty Frog disappeared,
and Boy-Don disappeared—
'Hello, bush folk.'
'GROAK, GROAK. GROAK, GROAK.' . . ."

It went on and on, with the girls and boys joining in, jumping round, *"'Groak, groak. Groak, groak . . .'"*

This new name "Boy-Don" caught on! It became the new fashion to say "Boy-Don," "Boy-Don," till now. Till now! . . .

Granny-May gave Mr. Burke a basket of things, saying it was just a few special mangoes, a melon, a pineapple, and some oranges. Mr. Burke drove off in his noisy horn blowing, and all three of them waved to him.

Granny-May and Miss Gee's house was clean, neat, and cool. They had an electric fan in a sitting-room ceiling. They took Boy-Don into a room with a single bed. He put his bag down and came out into the backyard that had lots of Joseph-coat crotons, masses of flowers blooming, lots of vegetables planted, and spaced-out trees. Miss Gee called him onto the back veranda. Everybody sat down and had iced lemonade. "Nicholas, you forgot to take your cap off," Granny-May said.

Boy-Don grabbed his cap, "Sorry, ma'am."

He tucked it in beside himself in the chair.

"And d'you always wear your cap with the front sideways, Nicholas?" Miss Gee asked.

"Not always, ma'am."

"So it is deliberate?"

"Sometimes, ma'am."

"Let's take him and show him the gardens," Granny-May said.

The sisters were proud of their many flowers, vegetables, and fruit trees. Boy-Don noticed the low, dwarfed coconut-palm trees bearing clusters of young coconuts. The trees were so low, a tall girl or boy could reach up and pick a nut.

"Would you like a water coconut?" Granny-May asked.

"Yes, ma'am, I would."

And looking up, the tall Granny-May held and twisted a green young coconut till its stem broke. She chopped off the top, and Boy-Don drank the coconut water. He heaved a sigh of pleasure, grinned, and said, "Can I have the meat, ma'am?"

"With a little local wet sugar?"

"Oh, yes, yes!"

Granny-May had hardly chopped the nut open on the ground to expose its soft white jelly when Miss Gee came back with the sugar and a spoon. The wet sugar ran like syrup over the jelly coconut. Boy-Don scooped and ate it all up greedily while the two ladies watched.

Boy-Don rushed here and there in the yard. He held on to the fence of the chicken run, looking at the fowls inside it, and unexpectedly felt he'd seen everything. He looked around and saw Granny-May and Miss Gee doing little jobs in their gardens. Somewhere in his tummy Boy-Don felt a loneliness like a first day at school. He watched the rooster and hens in the chicken run for a bit. He walked slowly up to his granny. "Granny-May, can we go to the sea?"

"Oh, yes, yes, Nicholas. I was going to suggest it. Let's go now."

They had a short walk along the main road. In both directions in the distance, noisy horn blowing of the unseen banana trucks came to them. Granny-May and Boy-Don turned into a lane of very tall coconut palm trees. Suddenly an endless sea opened out before them, under endless sky.

Only two couples could be seen on the warm and bright white-sand beach. Sunlight poured down. The clear space of wide, wide sea was wonderful. Boy-Don threw himself down on the sand. He shoved his hands down into the loose, hot sand and let it run freely through his fingers. He wrenched his feet out of his sneakers. He looked down at the busy water around his legs. The waves rolled out onto the sand and rushed back.

"Granny-May? Take off your shoes and come in."

"I doubt that, Nicholas."

"Did you bring my swim trunks, ma'am?"

"Did you bring them with you in your bag from home?"

"I don't think so, ma'am." And Boy-Don rushed out of the water. He tore off his denim trousers and shirt and dropped them on the sand. In his little white briefs he hopped and threw himself chest down flat into the sea and began swimming about.

Granny-May stood at the edge of the water and watched her grandson enjoying himself like a lively little dolphin. He dived down, and she stood with drawn breath till he surfaced again. He waited for a biggish wave and jumped over it like a dog over an obstacle, and she smiled. He waited for another wave and deliberately let it wash over him, and she looked worried. He swam backward and let the waves dump him on the sand, and she was thrilled at how well her grandson swam and controlled his little body in the sea. And Boy-Don enjoyed feeling the big sea shoving him about without something there for him to bounce against. Again and again he played that game. But unexpectedly, once more he wanted company. He was used to having brothers in the sea with him. He missed them. Big Andy always gave him a swim out on his back. Or they all played at fighting off sharks in a lot of terror noise, or splashed each other crazily. Or they jumped waves together. Boy-Don felt enough was enough by himself in the water. He came out of the sea, wanting to lie down on the sand and not talk. But Granny-May was all over him, drying him down with a towel and going on about what a wonderful swimmer he was.

"Andy and Hannah are both better'n me, ma'am."

"Better swimmers?"

"Yes. Much, much! They'll swim out to our beach rock in the sea and jump down into the deep water. I can't do that."

"I should hope not. That must be dangerous. Must be."

"Only one thing, though, ma'am, I can do better than all of them."

"So what's that?"

"I'm best at drawing and making rhymes."

"Drawing and making rhymes?"

"Yes, ma'am."

"That's two things. You're not good at arithmetic, Nicholas."

Boy-Don smiled. "No, ma'am. That's my worst subject."

"And I found you out!"

Boy-Don grinned wider. "Yes, ma'am."

"So what d'you draw? And what d'you make rhymes about?"

"Oh, ma'am, I draw big, bad ugly dogs with terrible fangs and claws and eyes of fire. And, ma'am, they're sneaky dogs. Really sneaky!"

"Why bad, ugly dogs? Why not nice dogs?"

"I already have a nice dog."

"Well, why not draw a donkey or a cow?"

"A donkey is a beast of burden. A donkey doesn't keep watch. A donkey doesn't have the chance to be bad like a dog."

"And a cow?"

"A cow can't be a friend or a terrible enemy like a dog."

"So I can see, Nicholas, you do think a lot about it all."

"No, ma'am. I only draw pictures with a

feeling. It's now when you question me I find I have an answer."

"So what about the rhymes you make?"

"My rhymes are about a silly story. You'd find them really silly."

"Did you bring one to show me?"

"Bring one, ma'am?" For a little bit Boy-Don was confused. Rap rhymes had rushed into his head—

> "In the lane at my trot of a jog,
> I met the one Mighty Frog.
> I looked him up,
> he looked me up.
> I looked him down,
> he looked me down. . . ."

"Yes. Did you bring one to show me?"

"No, ma'am. Nothing written down. But you wouldn't like it anyway. You wouldn't like it. You wouldn't." But the lines kept repeating in his head—"In the lane at my trot of a jog, I met the one Mighty Frog. . . ."

He knew it all by heart. He wished, wished he could right there perform this rap rhyme. But it was too silly. He couldn't, couldn't do it. If it was from a book, he'd recite it. But he made it all up himself.

"Next time will you bring me one of your rhymes and show me?"

Boy-Don was still doubtful. "Well, ma'am—I tell you what, I'll ask Andy. If Andy says it's okay, it'll be okay. It'll be fine."

"You're nice and dry now. Except for your wet underpants. Why not take them off and put your other things on?"

Granny-May was sitting on the sand, shaded by her broad straw hat with patterns of red roses on it. She took off her sunglasses and looked out over the sea. And Granny-May seemed full of dreams.

"I'll soon be back, ma'am."

Granny-May looked at Boy-Don and smiled.

Boy-Don breezed off, running, kicking up sand along the beach. He stopped, threw himself down and looked around him. He dug down hard with both hands, scooping up sand. His digging had the exact rhythm of his "Frog" rap rhyme. Nobody hearing him, Boy-Don performed "Mighty Frog" to his sand digging and the sound of the sea.

> *"In the lane at my trot of a jog,*
> *I met the one Mighty Frog . . .*
> *. . . Mighty Frog—* 'GROAK, GROAK.
> GROAK, GROAK.' . . ."

Afterward Boy-Don walked back along the beach, looking for any special thing the sea might have dumped. He looked up, and there was Granny-May walking toward him.

"Look, Granny-May! Look what I found!"

"Root of a little tree. Could make an ornament."

"Yes, ma'am. Polished up a bit more than the job sea and sand done already. It's a guava-tree root. Best it could make a small gig."

"A top?"

"Yes, ma'am."

"I'll put it in my bag. And the others? What's the others?"

Boy-Don held up a few shells, a big red back of a crab, and a small and slender piece of sea-polished timber. Granny popped the things into her bag and said, "We'd better be going. Miss Gee will have lunch ready and waiting." They sat down on the beach-hut bench. Granny-May wiped and brushed sand from his feet and between his toes. She put on his sneakers and laced them up. All this looking after made Boy-Don cringe. He hated it. Did Granny think he was a baby? Eh? Could Granny ever know he was the real big Boy-Don?

At the house Miss Gee had a fresh white cloth on a table laid for lunch on the back veranda. The big mango tree shaded the veranda from the afternoon sun.

Boy-Don cooled his thirst with iced lemonade right away. And boy, was he hungry! "Fresh fish run-down" was just what he wanted. The fish with chopped spring onions, garlic, tomatoes, pepper, and other seasoning had been added to coconut milk boiled to a curdle. Simmered with everything to a reddened rich gravy sauce, the "run-down" looked terrific. Served with yams, boiled green bananas, dumplings, okra, and spinachlike calaloo, the fish meal went down like best food at a feast. Then the skinned ripe bananas, baked with butter, brown sugar, and nutmeg, ended a meal when parts of a boy still wanted to continue.

Lunch over, Boy-Don drifted around the backyard. He passed the beds of flowers and the vegetable garden mixed with small coconut trees. Walking on, he saw that the place was an enormous land compared to his own backyard. Orange and grapefruit trees were here. Breadfruit and mango trees. Nutmeg and pimento-berry trees. Tall and skyward coconut trees. A cluster of sugarcane. Banana, plantain, coffee trees. All sorts of trees were spaced out here. Almost every tree was bearing fruit or was in blossom. Wondering, looking, thinking, Boy-Don heard Granny-May's voice break through, calling him. He turned around, answered, and ran back to the house.

In their sitting room, under the spinning fan of the ceiling, the two sisters were comfortably seated. Granny-May told Boy-Don this was no time of day to be out in the sun. She made him sit down on the sofa. She told him to stay there and rest himself. The cat came in and snuggled himself up at the other end of his sofa. Miss Gee asked Boy-Don questions about how he was getting on at school. He answered Miss Gee in ways it seemed to him he might please her. And that seemed to work. Miss Gee used to be a music teacher. She told Boy-Don she'd play the organ for him later. Then, except for the fan, the place went quiet.

Boy-Don began to think how much he'd like to draw. He remembered he had nothing to draw with. Then he noticed Granny-May and Miss Gee were asleep! Fast asleep! All this was odd, really odd, Boy-Don thought. The sisters fell asleep like this every afternoon, but Boy-Don didn't know. He kept looking at the two ladies, wondering if they were dead. They weren't really dead. But they were odd. And he couldn't go away. Granny-May put him to sit there on the sofa. If only he could do something. But he couldn't draw, couldn't think up rap rhymes, couldn't play with his dog Browndash or Rhino or Goaty. He couldn't talk, couldn't perform to his brothers and sister. And—a week! Here for a week! A whole, whole week! Loneliness, that sad loneliness of a first day at school came again and was heavy in Boy-Don's tummy. The whole inside of the room, the buzz of the spinning fan, the quiet curtains, the quiet tables and chairs, all was unfriendly. He sat up to pick up the cat. He'd almost touched the lovely black-and-white cat when it leaped up and rushed out of the room.

It was such a silly, stupid, baby thing to do. Yet here he was crying. Boy-Don was crying. He kept thinking of Browndash, Goaty, and

Rhino. But he didn't stop crying.

Granny-May and Miss Gee slept till the sun moved and it was cooler. He tried to conceal he'd been crying but couldn't. He just couldn't explain why he had become so sad and tears kept streaming down his face. He could only say, "I don't know. I don't know why I cry. I don't want to cry. But here I am crying."

The two sisters were really surprised and concerned. Miss Gee said, "Shall I play the organ for you? Would you like that?"

"I don't think it'll help, ma'am."

"Shall I sing some children's songs for you?"

"They make me think of other things, ma'am."

"Shall I tell you a story?"

"Yes—if it's about bad dogs."

"Well—can't say I know any of those."

Granny-May said, "Would you like a glass of lemonade?"

"Yes, thanks, ma'am." Boy-Don drank, and

the tears continued to come.

Granny-May went on. "Would you like us to go for a walk around the yard land at the back?"

"We can try."

All the walking around the land and the pointing out of different trees and birds did not stop Boy-Don's crying.

"You'll have to pull yourself together, Nicholas. You're here for a week. You'll have to give yourself a chance. You wake up in the morning and you'll see it's all different. You'll be your bright self again."

Tears gushed down Boy-Don's face more quickly. He wished, wished Granny-May would stop trying to find a way to make him want to stay. He couldn't say it to himself that staying was like staying in a tomb. He couldn't admit just thinking of going to bed one night here made him want to die. To die! He wanted, wanted the voices, noises, smells, everybody, everything, and all the goings on at his house so much that it hurt. It hurt badly, badly.

Granny-May held her handkerchief to his nose and asked him to blow. Then she wiped his face. "Can't you tell me how you really feel?"

"I can't, ma'am. I really can't. I don't know is nearest answer."

"D'you feel ill?"

"No, ma'am. Not really. Crying like this I just feel silly and stupid and bad, ma'am. But I can't stop myself."

Looking at him, Granny-May went on. "Nicholas, you know you'll have to stop crying, don't you?"

"All the time I'm trying."

"Well, you're here for a week. We're going to have a nice, nice time. I have plans made for us."

Boy-Don looked away. Tears came down in a new and stronger stream. "Plans made for us"—whatever, whatever they were—it frightened him, it hurt him. That odd belly pain took away his strength. It put a hold on him and made him helpless. It made him know he'd be carried off away into loneliness and loneliness. Boy-Don sobbed. He really felt foolish. He didn't know he could feel such a lost, lost boy and such a baby.

Granny-May was cross. She was concerned. She was worried. But mostly she was sad Nicholas was so unhappy. She stooped down. Face to face, she took Boy-Don's sobbing face into her hands lovingly and said, "Nicholas, Nicholas, you are with Granny-May. You are here with me. You will feel better. We're going to have a nice, nice time."

"We should, ma'am. We should. And I'm spoiling it."

"Never mind. You'll soon feel better. You'll see."

"My eyes must be red, ma'am. My eyes red?"

"I'm afraid your eyes are red. They've been flooded on and on for some time now! But never mind." She hugged him, kissed him, and wiped his face again. "Never mind. You'll feel better tomorrow."

That word "tomorrow" was a terror rather than a comfort to Boy-Don! He couldn't stay till tomorrow! The word was like a sentence for him to be locked away in prison. Tears came down freely. He looked up at his granny with his wet, tear-sodden face. "How you going to stop me crying, ma'am? How you going to stop me?"

His granny certainly didn't say, I'll see that you get back home tonight. She said, "We go back and play cricket. Would you like to play cricket?"

And he answered, "We can try, ma'am. We can go and try."

"Come on."

The sun had been going away gradually. Tree shadows were longer now. At the house Granny-May brought out a rubber ball with her dead husband's cricket bat and wicket. She began bowling underarm to Boy-Don's batting. His tears came with sobbing. They had to give up the game with Granny-May saying, "Nicholas, you'll have to stop this crying.

You'll have to stop it. Otherwise I'll just have to put you to bed and lock you up early, by yourself."

Granny-May's threats held out and promised nothing else but a stay for the night, and perhaps longer. His awful pain got worse. His tummy was heavy and strange and made him weak. It was very, very sad how he felt alone and lost in a strange, wild place and there was no way ever to get home again.

Washed in tears, full of apologies, eating at the table in the dining room with Granny-May and Miss Gee, Boy-Don felt helpless. Then a truck stopped down at the gate. Its ten-trumpets-fanfare horn was sounded! Going home with empty truck from his last trip, it was Mr. Burke coming up to the front veranda.

"Just a friendly stop," he said, "to see if Boy-Don would like me to take a message home for him."

"A message? A message?" tears vanished, Boy-Don said, looking around at everybody on the veranda now, "Can I go? Can I go back with Mr. Burke? His truck is empty, ma'am. All empty! Mr. Burke, sir, can I come back with you? Granny-May, can I go?"

Granny-May's disappointment was swallowed in silence before she said, "How will you explain your short, short stay with us?"

"I won't, ma'am. I won't. And everybody will know it's my fault." Tears gone, Boy-Don was wide-eyed, pleading with his granny.

"Get your bag. Next time I will come and stay with you."

"Yes, ma'am. Yes, ma'am. Do that. Me, Browndash, Goaty, and Rhino will take you out walking."

The big glow of orange sun was sinking behind the sea when Boy-Don arrived home. Astounded, unable to believe that he'd actually come back home on the first evening, everybody came quickly onto the veranda and stood speechless. Bag hanging from his shoulder, cap on his head turned sideways, Boy-Don shoved Granny-May's quickly written letter into his mother's hand and disappeared.

"Boy-Don, come back here!" Mrs. Wallman demanded. "Come right back here and tell what happened!"

Boy-Don came out again. He busily searched in one pocket after the next, as if he had much, much more important matters to deal with. "Mama," he said, "please can I go and do something very, very urgent? And first I must change my clothes."

"Stay right here and talk! You went off to Granny-May for one week. Why have you come back first night?"

Boy-Don was quick and confident. "All's in the letter, ma'am. All's in the letter."

"Mr. Bigshot couldn't bear spending even one night away from home," Hannah said, "let alone a week."

"I'm dying to know what happened," eight-year-old Mark said. And he joined his tickled sister, not able to stop tittering.

"The brief note only says, 'Nicholas had a severe attack of homesickness,'" their mom said. "And, 'A longer letter will follow.'"

"Homesickness!" Hannah screamed. Mark rolled about in fits.

"Boy-Don," Mark said, "did you vomit?"

The children screamed out laughing before their mom could say, "Stop it! Stop it!"

"After all that elaborate preparation—and fuss—to get away," Hannah said. "Didn't I say you'd have nothing interesting to say when you got back? Didn't I?" Hannah couldn't stop herself laughing. "Didn't I, Boy-Don? Eh? Answer me."

Mark said, "I wish I'd been invited, don't you, Hannah?"

"I bet you," Hannah said, "I bet you he cried. Did you cry at Granny-May's, Boy-Don? Did you start crying?"

Boy-Don only gave Hannah a bitter, glaring look.

"Come on now," their dad, Headmaster Mr. Wallman, said. "Give him a break. He'll talk when he's ready. You will, won't you Boy-Don?"

"Yes, Dad."

"Then, come closer. And say what happened."

Boy-Don went and stood beside his dad. "Well, sir—at first it was exciting. Then—then, it wasn't."

"Why wasn't it exciting anymore?"

"Well—Granny-May and Miss Gee went to sleep. Fast asleep."

Hannah screamed, "Went to sleep? And left you?"

"Yes. Went to sleep. And had me in the room to go to sleep as well. And I couldn't sleep. And I couldn't leave the room. I didn't want to disobey."

A situation like this had not been considered. Everybody now listened keenly to Boy-Don.

The fascinated Hannah said, "For how long? How long did they put you to bed for?"

Mark couldn't hold back his giggle. But Boy-Don took no notice. "I was in the room watching them sleep for a long, long time."

"And what happened?"

"It was like Granny-May and Miss Gee were dead—or dying all the time. And I was left all alone. And I missed everybody. I missed everybody at home so, so much. And it was like I known everybody here a long, long time ago. And I wouldn't find you again. And it was sad, sad!"

"And did you cry?"

"Dad, please will you ask my sister not to bother me?"

"Sister, don't bother your brother. And— so—you came back home, first night?"

"Dad, I couldn't bear not coming back— this very, very night."

"Well—you're back home."

Boy-Don didn't dare look at his dad. A terrible weight had been lifted off him. He felt all a new man again. And he said, "Thank you, Daddy. Thank you, sir." And Boy-Don disappeared as swiftly as he could, with Browndash behind him. He went to see Goaty, in a little outhouse in the backyard. Goaty was lying down chewing her cud. Still chewing, happy to see him, she looked at him, then looked away and listened to his voice. Boy-Don stroked his goat, saying all about how he was back. Then he and his dog rushed off again. At the pigpen, Rhino also was lying down. Happy to see Boy-Don, the pig grunted specially. Boy-Don stroked Rhino, telling him all about how he was home again. Then, in the dusk of the thickening night, Boy-Don and Browndash ran around and around the yard, playing.

Boy-Don felt he was outside of the family right now. He knew everybody was cross with him. He stayed away from talking to anybody.

Lights had come on in the house. Except for Andy, everybody was sitting on the front veranda, getting the little cooler night breeze. Andy sat under a light in the sitting room, reading. Boy-Don came to him and whispered, "Andy, please, can you announce to everybody I want to perform?"

Big brother Andy held the book down. He stared straight into his little brother's face. "You mean you want to have a go at making things up with everybody, don't you?"

"I—I didn't say that."

"But you want to try and mend your day's bad-behavior damage? Right?"

"I'm not saying that."

"All the same, it's that you want to get back into everybody's good books. Isn't it?"

"Don't say that when you announce me." Boy-Don shook his head, staring back into Andy's face. "Don't, don't, don't say that."

"How much you going to pay me?"

"How much you charge?"

"I'm not cheap. D'you think I'm cheap?"

"I'm not a poor man. Do you think I'm a poor man?"

Andy chuckled and grinned. He got up, leaving his book on the table. He went straight out onto the veranda. "Announcement! Boy-Don would like to do a performance of his rap rhymes for everybody!"

"That's a piece of cheek!" Hannah said. "Does he think anybody's even speaking to him?"

"Hannah," Andy said slowly, "I am directing and presenting this show. Okay?" He looked around and saw Boy-Don standing in the doorway. At fourteen years old, Andy's voice was changing. He went for his big dramatic announcement. He threw his arms wide open and his voice was loud. *"For his family!"* Andy's voice went astray. His husky voice broke into a peculiar high note. Then it came husky again and ran into strange sounds, as he said, *"Our own Boy-Don performs his rap rhymes!"*

Nobody could hold back. A grin or smile on every face, everybody clapped.

The veranda lights weren't switched on. Its light was a reflection of lights from the sitting and bedrooms. Boy-Don stepped out, dancing, in the dim veranda light. Front of cap turned sideways over his ear, arms swinging in rhythm, head nodding, he was into it.

"'Hello,' I said to the donkey I saw.
He said, 'Boy-Don, HEE-HAW,
HEE-HAW, HEE-HAW, HEE-HAW!'

"I saw the horse with his long face
just by a nose won his race.

"I saw my very own hog
sitting there on a log.
I said, 'Hog—so you really think?'
Hog said, 'OINK? OINK? OINK?
    OINK?'"*

Everybody clapped.

"Do it again!" Hannah yelled. "Do it again."

Boy-Don looked around to see if everybody agreed.

"Yes, yes!" Mr. Wallman said. "Encore! Encore!"

Not only once, but twice, arms swinging, head nodding, Boy-Don had to do his "Hee-haw, Long Face" again.

"Do 'The Mongoose,'" Andy said.

"'The Mongoose'?" Hannah said.

"Yes," Andy said. "About the mongoose who comes to the fence—"

"And makes a noise," Hannah chipped in, "to get fowls confused so he can catch them!"

"As it is said by folk wisdom."

Hannah insisted, "We've all heard them at the fence or a little way off under cover, doing their terrible, shrill cry."

"Boy-Don?" Andy said, "you were working on your 'Mongoose' rap rhyme. Was it finished?"

"Long time."

"You'd like to do it?"

Arms swinging in rhythm, head nodding, Boy-Don was at it again.

> "Listen to the mongoose
>   Calling fowls out of henhouse.
>   'SHRISH-SHRISH-SHRISH,
>   SHRISH-SHRISH-SHRISH.
>   You are sweeter than fish.
>   Come on let me eat you up.
>   Come on be my sweet sup-sup!'

"Listen to the mongoose
Calling fowls out of henhouse.
'SHRISH-SHRISH-SHRISH,
SHRISH-SHRISH-SHRISH.
You are sweeter than fish.
Come on let me eat you up.
Come on be my sweet sup-sup!'"

"Again! Again!" Boy-Don heard, and performed his "Mongoose" rap rhyme three times.

His dad embraced him. His mom embraced him. Hannah embraced him. Andy and Mark didn't embrace him. But he knew, Boy-Don well knew, everything was all right again at home with everybody.

SON-SON FETCHES THE MULE

Animals have another sense, it would seem. They know when you are a child, and they love you for being a child. An animal will let a child pet him, boss him, and even handle him up-side down, in any crazy or awkward old way, like he was dead. He would love it and give himself up to it, limply and totally. But there are other times when an animal hates it if a boy gets the better of him. That happened to Son-Son. Just fetching the mule, Son-Son found himself in trouble with him. Not ex-pecting it, he saw the good-good behavior of the work mule was all spite, all vicious teeth and hooves kicked up in the air. And now Son-Son had the mule to fetch as a regular morning job, before school.

Yesterday—first time he started this new job—the mule gave him a really bad time. He played bad man. Could have damaged him! And nobody must ever know—*must ever know*—he couldn't handle Maroontugger, couldn't deal with him. Son-Son knew it and saw it: This job was his job. He must do it by himself.

Like yesterday, today was an everyday, warm, tropical early morning. Son-Son carried a coil of rope over his shoulder. His dad had told him to carry it. He should use the rope to make a halter around Maroontugger's head before he untethered him.

Son-Son came alone into the field of high grass. Much more excited than worried, he felt good. And he looked good. He wore his long-fronted white cap, short-sleeved floral shirt, short trousers, and his sandals. He walked under one of the coconut-palm trees that stood scattered about. Even when his sandals and toes quickly got wet with dew from the grass and weeds, he didn't mind. Son-Son took no notice of the morning sunlight or the tree shadows. He took no notice of noisy birds fluttering in trees, doing peep-peeps, squawk-squawks, coo-coos, or just straight singing. Son-Son's job made him walk nippily on, eyes ahead. Everything about him made him look purposeful.

In truth, Son-Son was thinking he liked the business of helping his dad. It made him feel grown up. But best, really, it was great to handle and ride the big mule totally on his own. He'd handled Maroontugger before, lots of times, though not by himself, till yesterday. They knew each other well. Yet when he came to take Maroontugger in for work yesterday, the mule treated him like a stranger. The mule put on a bad, bad face. Tried to attack him! He had to jump quick, away from the mule's kicks! And he wouldn't let him get the loop of rope round his long head; he wouldn't let him get on his back to ride him home; then he kicked up and kicked up, trying to throw him off.

At one time yesterday he'd got worried his job was taking him too long. And he'd figured it out that the mule didn't at all like a ten-year-old taking him in for work. Then he'd also seen that it wasn't anything about *him* that Maroontugger disliked. The mule worked too hard. And after all, who could blame him trying to get a day off? But a job was a job. He had to show Maroontugger that he had a job to do, just as he, Son-Son, had a job to do as well. And bad and vicious as the mule was, he had to take him in for work.

Son-Son came on into the field lit with morning sunlight. He saw Maroontugger. He was still feeding—head down in the field of high grass and scattered trees. Son-Son stopped. He watched the mule. He saw Maroontugger and yesterday's terrible mule-madness went from him. Evaporated! Son-Son felt good. It was great to be there alone with this big, elephant-looking reddish fellow. He listened to the mule's greedy and noisy chewing. The huge jaws with half circles of axelike grabber teeth chewed grass again and again. The working of the big jaws made a noise like a grinding in an empty barrel. Son-Son's eyes widened and shone. "Jees!" he thought. "Terrific! Terrific how the grinding of the strong and loud eating has no good manners! No good manners at all!"

In his friendliest voice, Son-Son said, "Good mornin', Maroontug! Good mornin'!"

The mule lifted his head, tossed his long ears forward, and stopped chewing. His steady eyes watched Son-Son. And Son-Son couldn't guess that in the straight look the mule said, "Oh! So that's it! It's you again. The boss sent you again. You the boy to take me in for work! Well, we'll see! We'll see about that, won't we?"

Son-Son grinned. "Ahright, Maroontugger? Between we, you an' me the tops, you know!

Ahright?" The mule's long ears, tossed forward over his eyes, reminded him of his own long-fronted cap on his head. He walked forward. "Had a good night, Tugger-boy? Sleeping alone under the stars?" Son-Son stopped again, looking around, fascinated as he had been the morning before. The high grass had been eaten or trampled down in a circle, as much as the mule's rope would allow. Son-Son said, "So you eat an' eat all through the night! No sleep, then? You just eat an' eat right through till daylight? Gosh! I couldn't do that. I couldn't eat all night like that, Tugger-boy." He looked at the mule's huge bulge of two-sided belly. "Look at your belly! Jees! Look at you! I bet you the greediest an' strongest mule ever. I bet you could pull away any great house. And could run away pulling any busload of people! Or any high-up-loaded banana truck! Listen, listen, Maroontug! I just get a great new idea.

"Every day's always so, so sunny an' hot. Suppose one day—one day—when it really raining hard, I take you fo' a wet gallop, an' you take me fo' the wet-wet ride? Eh? How about that? Aroun' an' aroun' the big pasture land fo' a good, wet, rainy gallop, when the two of we soak-soak to the skin, dripping? Eh? Naw? Dohn like it? Okay. I think again.

"You always working. An' I always going school. Suppose one day—one day—I dohn go school an' you dohn go work, an' we just team up? We team up big-big. We go cricket match. You walk beside me. We walk like man an' man. No rope on your head or anything. An' then we stand together an' watch play ball. Just watch! An' I explain the whole game to you. Then, then, when I have my best-best favorite thing—which is my barbecue jerk pork an' dry bread—I get you some sugar. Naw? No good? Well—when I have my second best-best favorite thing—which is fried fish and fried dumplin', followed by cool ginger ale—I get you a pint a stout. Naw? I can see you woulda like rum. Noh. No rum. I cahn buy rum like that. But—all the same—Maroontug, I got to go to school. An' you got to go work. An' I must take you in. So I better."

The mule stood there all the time, staring. Son-Son walked up to him, taking the coil of rope from his shoulder. He reached up to put the rope around his head, and the mule's rebellion again was on. The meanest, wildest attacking look came over the mule's face. He flattened his ears back against his head. A swift dread in Son-Son's face said, Stop it! Stop-it! as the mule swung around and kicked out at Son-Son. Only swift evasive movement saved him. But mud from the mule's iron shoes had flown up to his cheek and stuck. The mule trotted off, turned his back, and stood at the full stretch of his rope, looking away.

Really cross, Son-Son was brisk. Wiping the soft blob of earth and grass from his cheek, he rushed up to the mule's face and shouted. "Maroontugger! What you think you playing at? Eh? What you think you doing? You think you all wild, stupid, bad, and fool-

fool! Why you behaving like you have no train-
ing? An' no respect? You want a good friend
get rough an' careless with you? You wahn me
beat you? You wahn feel my whip hand? I tell
you—dohn change me. You well know, you a
good trained worker. An' I Son-Son"—tapping
his chest with his fingers—"I the man who
must take you in. Take you in fo' work. This
very mornin'. Understan'? Ahright? So no
more wild foolishness! You hcar me? Good. I
going to put the rope around your head, softly,
softly. Know that. So easy now. Easy . . . Steady
now, boy . . . Steady. Easy now . . ."

As Son-Son again was about to slip the wide
loop of rope over Maroontugger's head, the
mule bared his enormous teeth and clapped
his jaws together near Son-Son's face. Horror-
struck, "Stop et!" he bawled. His screaming
rage echoed through the field and panicked
the mule. He tossed his head in the air, backed
off, turned around, and walked away. Again he
stood with his rear end turned on Son-Son, as
if to say, "Go away. I don't want to see you.

Don't want anybody collecting me. Don't want any work. Sweating, sweating all day, pulling logs uphill, pulling, pulling . . ."

Son-Son felt upset and looked it. It hurt him that Maroontugger didn't take him as a friend. "How can he not take me as a friend?" he whispered. He looked out up and down along the track at the side of the land. He stood still in the grassy field. If his dad came after him, there'd be trouble. His dad knew he'd handled Maroontugger before. He might forget it was never by himself—except yesterday. It would be hard to make his dad believe Maroontugger wanted to hurt or scare him off. And—he had other morning jobs to do.

Unexpectedly Son-Son felt better. He knew—he just knew—it wasn't himself Maroontugger disliked. For sure, it was hard work the mule wanted a rest from. True-true, the mule's job was sweaty, terrible. Two other mules tugged and pulled timber logs up to the sawmill with Maroontugger. Even so, cutting up the hillside was neither fun nor an easy game to play. And whether his dad worked Ma-roontugger himself or not, the mule went up-hill-downhill, all day long in the hot-hot sun.

His dad never took things easy himself. His dad gave way to nothing. His dad worked him-self as hard as he worked his mule. Partner to another man using the electric saw, he ripped and ripped massive tree trunks into timber. By himself with a handsaw, axe, or machete, he cut and chopped away the tree limbs and branches. He cleared away branches and heaved logs. At sundown, when he and Ma-roontugger came home each night, his dad's clothes were full of hot-sun smell and sweat and wood sap. And when he changed clothes, sawdust fell off his shirt and out of his cuffs and boots.

Son-Son began to imagine everybody else getting on with their morning jobs at his yard. He imagined his mom at the kerosene stove getting breakfast. His oldest brother had fed the chickens and now fed the pigs. His sister tidied the house. His smaller brother had got the barrel more than half full with water from the standing pipe on the village road. His dad had milked the cow. His dad would soon be sitting on the back steps, sharpening his axe and machete. First to have breakfast, his dad could be having it any time now, giving half of it to the dog, Judoboy. All that meant he'd soon be ready to saddle up Maroontugger. He would soon want to wrap and sheath his machete and axe and then fasten them against the saddle before he rode out of the yard, with Judoboy following.

Unexpectedly Son-Son heard a voice. "Havin' a spot of trouble, Son-Son, mi boy?"

Son-Son swung his head around quickly and saw Mr. G. He was a short man in a straw hat, short sleeves, and sandals, carrying a bag around his shoulder and a machete in his hand. On his way to his plot of land, Mr. G had come down the lane.

"Maroontugger trying play bad man with me, sir."

Mr. G chuckled. "Yeh, I see that." He

stood. He and the mule looked at each other. "Son-Son, do your job. Go right on, Son-Son. Handle him!" Mr. G watched. Then he strolled away.

Son-Son began walking up to the mule. He had a new feeling. He always knew he was the mule's boss. But now, unexpectedly, that feeling had grown much bigger. A big and bold confidence came more and more into his steps and whole body. It flowed in him like a strange, magic light. The mule looked away and stood quietly, peacefully. The fearless feeling Son-Son had was terrific. He knew he had grown taller, into something almost as muscular and strong and tough as his daddy. He knew this new light in him subdued the mule. He knew Maroontugger couldn't move and wouldn't move.

The mule just stood there, calm-calm, letting himself be handled. "Tuggerboy? You see how it easy? See how it easy-easy? Nice an' easy?" Son-Son had put the big loop of rope around Maroontugger's head. He then brought it against each side of the face, all the way down to the corners of the mouth. He tied the dangling rope on one side, took it across above the nose, tied it, drew a long loop for reins and tied it the other side of the mule's jaw. All the time, Son-Son looked like a midget harnessing an elephant. He completed the halter making, feeling good. He stroked Maroontugger's neck. "You see is ahright. Ahright an' easy? Eh? Ahright an' easy? Good boy."

Son-Son led the mule to the post in the ground where he was tethered. He loosed the rope.

Son-Son really thought his battles with Maroontugger were all over. But Maroontugger knew different. Maroontugger's head kept a lot more secret spite to force Son-Son to leave him alone. As Son-Son tried to get up onto the mule's back, the new tricks started. Every time Son-Son tried to clamber up, Maroontugger gently eased himself away like a sideways dance. And Son-Son came down again, right on his own two legs. Over and over, holding on to the rope reins against the mule's shoulder, Son-Son heaved himself up; and each time, that smart sideways movement made him miss his mount and come down again. Finally Son-Son chuckled with a sigh, saying "Tugger-boy—okay. You've had your go. Now I'll have mine."

Son-Son led the mule and tied his head close against a coconut tree. Then, holding the end of the rope, he climbed up the tree trunk and lowered himself down onto the mule's back. Son-Son thought at last he'd won. He couldn't believe the mule kept an extra reserve store of badness saved up. The moment Son-Son drew that slippery knot he'd tied round the tree and loosed the mule, that was it! Maroontugger tugged his head, swished his tail, and jumped off, racing away like a wild bull, all crazy and malicious. The mule bolted on, going his own way, without control. Son-Son could not check him. Bobbing his head with a stubborn defiance, Maroontugger raced on, going deeper into the field. He galloped recklessly under trees, trying to knock his rider off. Son-Son ducked under branches, lying down on the mule's bare back like a North American Indian rider. His cap blew away. All the time now, he pulled and jerked and tugged at the mule's head as hard as he could, shouting, "Whoa! Whoa! Whoa, now! Whoa, Maroontugger! Whoa, boy!"

At last, pulling and holding him firmly now, Son-Son turned Maroontugger around and held him to a walking pace. Not even allowed to break into a trot, he was ridden all the way back across the field out onto the track and then the village road.

Son-Son rode home into his yard on the big mule. He dismounted and tethered him, to await saddling up by his dad. The smell of brewed coffee, fried fish, and breadfruit roasting on the woodfire made Son-Son realize how hungry he was.

He went into the kitchen and couldn't believe how everything was normal. And nobody said anything about taking too long fetching the mule. Nobody even mentioned that he'd lost his cap. And he certainly would say nothing about it.

Nobody was ever going to say he couldn't manage Maroontugger. Nobody was even going to know the mule gave him a hard time. Yet as he ate breakfast, Son-Son knew the struggle with Maroontugger wasn't over. But he was ready. He was ready. Always he was going to let that mule understand—Son-Son was tall-tall.

THE FUTURE-
TELLING LADY

"Neil, we almost there now," his mother said. She sat up front beside his father, who was driving the car.

"Really great country drive, Mamma!"

"Cahn believe we never take you this way's far as this before," his father said.

"Never. And the road signs say we leave MoBay a hundred miles behind us. As you did say the distance was."

"Yes. Our town Montego Bay is a bit behind us now."

"What you going to tell Mother Eesha, Neil?"

"Me, Mamma?"

"Yeahs—you."

Neil's face took on its fierce, fighting look. "Me wohn have anything to say to her. You and Dad brought me here." His dad stopped the car at the side of the village road. They were beside a neatly kept hibiscus hedge with arbors of slender, flowering branches inside the yard. All the windows of the car were completely down in the warm, bright Saturday morning.

"Mother Eesha may want to question you a little. Jus' to talk to you a little. Jus' for you to say something."

Neil did not want to come for this appointment. He didn't want any going on about his "problem." He folded his arms and looked down. "I'll say 'Good morning, Mother Eesha.'"

His father chuckled. "Neil, you know we're only trying our best to help you."

"Help me with what, Dad? A bit of swi-swi magic business? Beats me how you really seem to go for this sorta thing."

"Why d'you have this attitude, Neil?" his

103

mother asked in a worried but kind voice.

Neil shifted about. His face went taut. All huffy, he spat out, "I'll tell you why. A boy at school seen Mother Eesha. Since then he's gone really stupid!"

"How has he gone stupid?"

"Brian Rowe used to come out good with math and some history. Since he seen Mother Eesha, he's nothing but a nitwit!"

"Tell us why him seeing her affects you badly."

"Mamma, 'cos it looks too much like swi-swi man Obeah business."

"No, no, no, Neil. Mother Eesha's nothing to do with witchcraft. Mother Eesha's a healer. Big, big difference."

"Cahn say I like any of it."

"What did Brian Rowe tell you?"

"He didn' tell me. I jus' hear him carrying on."

"Saying what, Neil?"

"All about how Mother Eesha tells him about his future. All the rubbish about every name having what she calls a 'Name-Story.' Kind of message she sees in a name. Coming in a poem. And all about his future, Mamma. I dohn wahn to know about my future."

"I'd be intrigued. All ears to know my future. Was his future bad, then? Wasn't it good?"

"From what Brian Rowe said, she didn' talk straight."

"Can you remember any of what she seen in his name?"

"Lots a nonsense about how his name gets him pestered 'cos he's become famous. And his name also gets him exposed, 'cos he's become scandalous."

"Sounds as if he grew up and became a baddy. And gets himself in the newspaper."

"No, ma'am. No. Not necessarily a baddy. It could mean jus' 'cos he's famous, whatever he does makes news in the papers."

"What was the matter with Brian?" Neil's dad asked. "What did he see Mother Eesha for?"

Neil shook his head. "Dohn know, Dad. Never asked."

"I think we better go in now."

"Dad—can we wait a minute?"

"What for?"

"Might as well tell you the rest of what Brian Rowe said."

After all his resistance, Neil was ready to talk properly. No wonder his parents looked at each other in disbelief. Without looking at his watch, his dad said, "Yeh. Okay. We have some time."

"Well—Brian tells us that—without anybody telling—Mother Eesha was right on with what he likes doing best. He said she knew. She jus' come out with it. And she read him something from Brian's own grown-up diary. His own grown-up diary! Ma'am, did you know she could do that?"

"Neil, we're taking you because Mother Eesha helps children."

"Yes, Neil," his dad said. "She's known for that."

"I'll tell you. You see, Brian's crazy—crazy about bridges. The only other thing he does is draw airplanes. But tha's jus' a sideline. Always, always he's drawing bridges. And reading about bridges. And—gets his parents to take him to see a bridge anywhere, everywhere."

"So what did she *see* in Brian's future diary?"

Neil wanted to remember as correctly as he could. His parents didn't take their eyes off him. Right away there, in the back of the car, his face took on the look of really hard concentration. He started slowly. "All about—writings, about going to see bridges. Going to see—one-arch bridges to bridges with well over twenty arches. Some writing about—how at first he merely liked bridges. Then it was their structure in the air, over water or over a valley, that got him. And that was when he became a builder of bridges. And—some writing about—about excitement seeing a wonderful hidden-away little old bridge. Writing about—how and why a mossy one-arch wood-and-

107

stone country bridge lasted three hundred years. Also some writing about—standing, looking to see how a bridge fits in the landscape under the sky. And writing about—a great sensation, feeling the wood, the stone, the iron, that made a bridge. Writing about—scrambling down slopes to see the underbelly of a bridge. Seeing how a bridge stands comfortably in water, while some of it is in the air and some of it resting on the land." Neil looked at his parents.

"That was good!" Neil's dad said. "Really very good to remember all that."

As if he was confused and unsure of his feelings, Neil kept a straight face and did not smile.

"Oh, Neil!" his mother said. "I've never heard you do anything like that so, so well! To think of remembering all that! Very, very good!"

Neil's story made his mother want to tell him something. But she wasn't sure it would help anything. She decided to stay quiet. She and Neil's dad had never told him about the unusual stories they knew about the work of Mother Eesha's mother. Mother Eesha's mother was famous for her use of herbs, her special bark and herbal baths, use of oils, and of course her healing touch.

Neil's dad and mom knew many stories about people who came to see Mother Eesha's mother for healing. And they'd been cured when doctors had given them up as incurable. They knew stories about the dumb boy who made no sounds at all except when Mother Eesha's mother touched him and talked to him. With her hand resting on him, the dumb boy would start singing, making the strangest of sounds. And from nowhere, dogs would arrive, gather around and howl with him as he sang. They knew stories about how a donkey would start braying when she asked it to say something. But they never tried to convince Neil of anything concerning these stories.

Mother Eesha had inherited a caring for the sick from her mother, and she had come along finding her own sympathy and skills. The community depended on her for her particular gifts and help.

"We better go in now," Neil's dad insisted.

The car turned in and drove along the driveway. Mother Eesha's relatives lived in freshly painted bungalows on both sides of the driveway. Her land really rolled on into twenty acres. The land kept animals. And it was planted out with coconuts and bananas, with mango and other fruit trees and plots of vegetables. Usually it wasn't only people in cars who came to see Mother Eesha. People also came on bicycles, on the backs of horses, mules, and donkeys, and on foot. Today was quiet.

Neil stood in the sunlight, fascinated, looking at Mother Eesha's unusual house. A neat-looking bungalow, circular, thatched, with a veranda all around, it gave Neil a pleasure just to see it. While Neil was all taken up with looking, two young women came up to his parents. And—dressed in purple gowns and purple headbands—the young women took the family inside, into the reception room.

Beside everything in the room, Neil's gaze fell right away on two things: a large, uncovered glass jar full of plain water, and a big painting of seven circles of colors linking with each other.

Mother Eesha came in. She greeted the family, then said to Neil, "I noticed you were looking at the painting."

Neil's voice came out faintly, "Yes, ma'am."

Everybody looked at the painting now as Mother Eesha herself looked at it and explained, "Well, it's my idea of the seven days of the week. White for Sunday, red for Monday, orange for Tuesday, yellow for Wednesday, green for Thursday, blue for Friday, and purple for today, Saturday. Every day, for my work, I wear my Day-Color. As you see, today, Saturday, I wear my purple."

Neil stood wide eyed, looking at this impressive lady in her wide-sleeved purple gown and purple head wrap. Neither tall nor short, neither black nor white, neither yellow nor red, Mother Eesha with her brown skin and her soft voice seemed like a union with everybody. Soon, swiftly, they were at the other side of the house, in a spacious open-windowed room with wickerwork furniture. The family sat with Mother Eesha around a low, glass-top circular table.

"Why the worry about Neil?" Mother Eesha asked.

"Ah, Mother Eesha!" Neil's mother said, sighing. "Our beautiful son here steals things. He takes other children's things. And sometimes brings them home. A watch, books, pens, money, a Swiss pocketknife, a calculator—things like that! Things that often he already has! And also, he doesn't always tell the truth. Fortunately—so far—we managed to quieten things with parents. We keep in touch with his headmaster. But Mother Eesha, you never know, do you, when a parent is going to be totally not approachable?"

"And punishing him doesn't seem to do

much at all," Neil's father said.

"Mother Eesha, punishing makes him worse!"

"And our doctor doesn't have a clue as to what to do to help."

"Goodness knows why he steals," Neil's mother said helplessly. "We are both honest people. We not rich. But we not poor. We can afford to buy Neil things. And we do. And he's not short of pocket money."

"Of course, this means we have to keep a sharp eye on Neil. We get him to take back everything he pinches."

"With a letter of apology from himself and one from us."

"Mother, you can understan', when things get to this stage, you do worry and wonder. Is he telling the truth? Is he hiding anything?"

"Which is so awful!" Neil's mother sighed again. "All the same, Mother, I have to say, Neil and his dad do have their arguments."

"The arguments only started when I tried to get him to take an ordinary bit of interest in sports. And I come to see he was never going to budge."

"Ah! But is it really an ordinary bit of interest?"

"Mother Eesha, the boy's by far too small for his age. He's too twiggy. Look at him! He looks underfed. And he's not. And trying to get him to take part in anything that'll help him to put on a bit of body is like trying to get a cat to have a swim."

"His father thinks Neil's too small for his age, but I dohn think so. I dohn think so at all. Neil's not bulky, that is so. But he's ahright. Neil's a good average for size. He's jus' not a cricket-loving, sport-loving West Indian boy! That is what he's not."

"Does Neil do anything he himself likes doing?" Mother Eesha asked.

"That boy'll sit alone for hours and hours playing games with his computer," his dad answered. "He needs no company, no companion. And you'll find him awake at night, reading science fiction. The answer is, Mother Eesha, Neil's very good at playing games, indoors, alone, playing with his computer."

Mother Eesha now kept her eyes on Neil's dad. She talked to him alone for a bit. It turned out that he'd always been a big boy for his age. Also, he was a passionate cricketer and played for a club. And he kept up with rugby and soccer playing around the world.

"So Neil is different?" Mother Eesha asked him.

"I wouldn' say it was worrying how different he was, but I'd say it makes a parent concerned."

"So there may be a way in Neil's nature that wants to bring something different into the family. Would you say?"

"Could be. Could be."

"You hadn't thought of that?"

"No. No."

Mother Eesha turned to Neil himself. "Neil?"

"Yes, ma'am."

"How d'you feel causing your parents all this worry?"

"Very bad."

"In what way, 'bad'?"

"Makes me feel I wish my parents were like some other parents, ma'am."

"D'you know why you cause them worry?"

"I'm too small for Dad's liking. And like a spite I wohn get bigger."

"Why d'you steal?"

Neil shuddered faintly. Then he suddenly smiled, but stayed silent.

"Why did you smile? What was the feeling that made you smile?"

"I shocked me, ma'am—that—that I suddenly know why—why I swipe things."

"Why, then, d'you swipe things?"

Neil sighed. "I—I wahn to have more, ma'am."

"More of what?"

"Jus' more. More of anything to make me bigger."

"You *will* get bigger! Your father here was once your size. And one day you'll be as big as he is."

Neil shook his head. "No, ma'am."

"What d'you mean, 'No'?"

"My dad was never my size, and I'll never be his size." Everybody laughed. "In your own way then, you'll get bigger," Mother Eesha said. Neil smiled again. She explained to Neil how she believed every name had a secret, personal Name-Story; and would he like to hear his personal Name-Story?

"Yes, ma'am," he said.

She told him she had to wait till it came into her head, in the form of a poem. She closed her eyes. And Mother Eesha was obviously thinking hard. Her lips began to move.

"Here's a Name-Story to be heard
about this special-special one word—
about a finder of what will fit,
who takes a problem and works at it,
who is warm or cool or hard like steel,
who carries the sound-sign that says NEIL!"

Neil was very thrilled. He grinned as if he couldn't stop. He looked as if he would ask

Mother Eesha to say his Name-Story again. But Mother Eesha said, "I cahn say it again. I don't remember it. But if you think, you'll remember it. And then you can write it down if you like."

Then Mother Eesha told Neil about the other secret and mysterious thing she found she could do for children. It was being able to read something that was written in their grown-up diary. Neil wanted a Grown-Up Diary Reading. So again Mother Eesha closed her eyes. That look of deep, deep thinking came over her face. And Mother Eesha said:

My Biggest Moneymaking Day

Hurray! Today I did it. Today I broke my best moneymaking record. For the first time, in one day I made one hundred thousand pounds buying and selling houses. Big and beautiful old houses!

People don't seem to know anybody can make lots of money. People don't know there are only a few rules to follow. But then, it was as I went

*along that I myself found my own six simple rules.
And what are those rules for my moneymaking?*

1. *To make a profit, you must really want to sell
   something.*
2. *You must like a line of business that supplies a
   demand.*
3. *Deep down, know you are going to succeed,
   come what may.*
4. *Be totally dedicated to your business.*
5. *Keep a sharp eye for the opportunity to expand.*
6. *Get your staff to like and enjoy working for you.*

Neil's eyes shone like stars, with an amazing, faraway look in them. "What a wonderful, wonderful secret!" he barely whispered. He looked at his parents, wishing they'd never tell this secret to anyone. Yet he said nothing to anybody—nothing at all.

When the family left Mother Eesha's place, the parents were well on their way to thinking up ways they could be different to Neil—particularly his dad.

119

Next, Wendy and her dad sat with Mother Eesha at the low, glass-top table.

Wendy's dad said, "Mother Eesha, Wendy won't eat. You see how flat and thin the poor child is. She's like two sticks walking. My lovely, lovely Wendy! She forces herself to eat. And jus', jus' brings it all up. I take her to see a specialist. But so far no change. None."

"How she gets on at school?" Mother Eesha asked.

"Perfect," her father said. "Wendy's usually tops in her year."

"And in her spare time? What she does?"

"Reads, reads, and reads adult books. Plays the piano. Or spends her time petting or over-caring for the cat. Slightest excuse and the poor animal has to put up with having a paw bandaged. Or taking medicine. For my part, she doesn't talk enough. Though she's good at it. And sometimes she amazes me how knowledgeable she is. Yet with her music, her scholarly ways, her helpfulness, Wendy's great company. But I have to say, I do wish there was more of the child about her."

"Wendy?" Mother Eesha said.

Wendy fluttered her eyelids and opened her eyes wide. "Yes."

"Why you wohn eat?"

Wendy scratched her head lightly, delicately. "I—I—I dohn know."

"No idea?"

"No."

"What does the empty, hungry feeling say?"

"It knows it's not a friend."

"Then how d'you put up with it?"

"I—I dohn know."

"You're very intelligent. You're a thinker. What reason you see for keeping a condition that's like an unwelcome friend?"

"Perhaps—somewhere—somewhere I feel there's too, too much cruelty in the world to grow up to."

"So?"

"So—I'd rather not grow up."

"Have you always understood it like that?"

"No."

"When did you understand it like that?"

"Jus' now."

"So your father didn't know?"

Two teardrops slowly swelled up and fell from Wendy's eyes. "No. I didn't know. He couldn't know."

Mother Eesha looked at Wendy with a deep sympathy. She waited, allowing Wendy to dry her eyes. "Okay now, Wendy?"

"Yes, ma'am."

"Tell me, don't you like reading stories for children?"

"Only when I mus', for school."

"What's it about grown-up books that makes you prefer to read them?"

"I started when I was nine years old and never stopped."

'Why you dohn jus' read children's books?"

"It's grown-up books draw me to them, ma'am."

"What in them draws you to them, Wendy?"

"West Indies history. And people stories. All bad and cruel and awful and terrible and sad. And ma'am, they kind of haunt and compel me to find and read more and more of them."

"And the feelings you described are the only feelings you find in the grown-up stories?"

"Yes, ma'am. Feelings—cruel and bad. Hurtful—and horrible. Like a sucking-down swampland that holds you in darkness to drown you."

"How, d'you think, a lot of grown-ups manage to live till they are old?"

Wendy was surprised. She glanced at Mother Eesha and gave a little smile. "I dohn know, ma'am. I really dohn know how they happen to manage that." Wendy laughed.

"It's your father who brings you. Why didn' your mother come too?"

"Mamma and Dad divorced. Mamma lives in Canada."

"You see her sometimes?"

"Yes, ma'am. But I dohn wahn to much."

"So you and Dad and the cat and the piano live alone?"

"We have a housekeeper with us—Miss Pimm. Miss Pimm is good to me. She teaches me to make a cake and iron properly."

"So you know now why you wohn eat?"

"I—I know. I dohn wahn to die because of Dad."

"So what you going to do?"

"I think—I think I'll know when I talk to Dad."

"And—you think—he'll understand?"

Wendy nodded. "Yes. Yes. I think so now."

Mother Eesha explained to Wendy how she believed every name had a secret, personal Name-Story. Wendy was keen to hear hers.

Mother Eesha closed her eyes. Wendy's Name-Story came like this:

> *"Here's a Name-Story to be heard*
> *about this special-special one word—*
> *called in bad temper and in soft*
> *whispers,*

called for a joke and to work,
called for a dance and to silence,
called to sobbing and to prize giving—
that WENDY! WENDY!
a real friend of the speechless many."

Wendy smiled a smile of someone who never expected to be surprised pleasantly. Her dad smiled too. He'd not seen such a happy look on Wendy's face for a long time.

Wendy wanted a Grown-Up Diary Reading as well. When Mother Eesha closed her eyes, this was what she said:

The Sick Donkey I Treated Practically Talked to Me

Today I felt both sad and happy at the same time. Nothing makes a vet feel better than seeing a sick animal recover. Janey the donkey was taken home today. Half dead when she came, today she looked oh so much better. So much more rounded up, with a strong, steady walk! But she didn't want to go.

Time to go and Janey looked at me with plead-ing eyes. Her look at me said, "Oh please, please, keep me here in your backyard, with its green grass and little houses. Don't let my owner take me away with him again. Don't let him take me. I'll die this time! Away from here, each day brings a heavy load on my back, in hot sun, seeming only up and up stony, hilly ground, on and on. I'll die under my burden of heavy load. I'll die this time!"

Sorry, Janey. A vet's job is to help animals, treat them, and get them well for themselves and their owners. But when an owner is poor and keeps an animal overworked, even when tired and ill, it is very, very sad.

Tonight, Janey, I'll support your rebellion. When I play the piano for myself tonight, I'll play my fa-vorite rebel song for you on your behalf.

Wendy cried. Her dad comforted her. She couldn't stop crying.

When they got into their car, he said, "Wendy, it's a long time since I've seen you cry. It's good to cry. It's good to cry like this. We understand this so much better now. Don't you feel so?"

"Yes, Dad. Yes . . ."

Day after day the Future-Telling Lady went on helping children and their parents. Her particular gifts helped them to see and understand their problems for themselves.

MR. MONGOOSE AND MRS. HEN

AUTHOR'S NOTE

When I was a child in my Jamaican village, I heard the story "Mr. Mongoose and Mrs. Hen" told with the characters of Sis Goose (as Mrs. Hen) and Brer Fox (as Mr. Mongoose). Later I discovered in London that the story was, in fact, an American folktale; it appears to have been first collected and published under the title "Old Sis Goose" (from BRAZOS BOTTOM PHILOSOPHY, *A.W. Eddins, 1923). My story, with its setting in Jamaica, develops the allegory of the original.*

Mrs. Hen was happy. Six fluffy and beautiful chickens had come under her, and all about between her feathers, after three weeks of sitting on her nest. Out in the big yard for the first time a proud mother, her six chicks peep-peeping around her. Mrs. Hen clucked all the time, protectively, caringly, happily, every chick close to her. But oh, unhappiness waited for her. Though the last idea Mrs. Hen would ever have was that somebody was somewhere all ready to turn her happiness into misery.

That Mr. Mongoose peeped through the fence and saw Mrs. Hen with her new chickens. And Mr. Mongoose weighed everything up. Mr. Mongoose looked to see who was about. Mr. Mongoose hid himself and waited for everything to be exactly the right moment.

There in her yard Mrs. Hen was totally taken up with mothering her fluffy first-day chicks. Mrs. Hen searched and clucked, calling her chicks to hurry and see who'd be the first to take any bits of food she'd found.

Mr. Mongoose, careful not to be seen,

strolled up into the yard as if he knew nothing would stop him. Then, with one straight reckless dash, Mr. Mongoose charged right into the middle of Mrs. Hen and her chickens. Everything feathers and panic and terror, mother and chicks hollered and scattered, screaming. Nippily, cockily as Mr. Mongoose came, he left again. Vanished! Was gone! Shattered and stunned as she was, Mrs. Hen turned here, turned there, calling her chicks together. In her terror Mrs. Hen moved quickly to the other side of her yard, with frightened chicks trying to keep close beside her.

Mrs. Hen comforted her chicks. She sat down. She got the chicks to nestle safely all around in her tummy feathers. But clucking, clucking, calling, Mrs. Hen knew one chick was missing. She knew—oh, she knew—Mr. Mongoose had gone off with one of her babies. Yet she couldn't stop calling. And that sound—that sound of Mrs. Hen's calling— was the sad sound of a distressed mother.

Unexpectedly a voice spoke to Mrs. Hen.

"Awful, isn't it? I know. I know how terrible it is."

"You do?" Mrs. Hen said, looking up and seeing Mrs. Ground Dove sitting on a low branch. "I'm shattered," Mrs. Hen went on. "Shattered. Thank you for saying something. Thank you so much."

"I saw it all," Mrs. Ground Dove said.

"You saw it happen?"

"I saw it happen."

"What then can I do? Oh, what can I do?"

"Nothing," Mrs. Ground Dove said.

Alarmed, Mrs. Hen said, "Nothing? Nothing I can do?"

"Nothing," Mrs. Ground Dove said. "I lost my whole family to that beast Mr. Mongoose."

"Your whole family?" Mrs. Hen gasped.

"My whole, whole family," Mrs. Ground Dove said. "And I tell you, I myself have to be careful. Have to be very careful. He's taken friends of mine. Taken them! And tried after me, too. Tried to turn me into feathers. Yes, he's tried."

"This is dreadful," Mrs. Hen said. "Dreadful. Do—do—if you hear, hear about anything—anything—that can be done, let me know. Please."

"I will. I will," Mrs. Ground Dove said, and flew away.

Next morning Mrs. Hen made sure she didn't take her babies to the same side of the fence as yesterday. But soon, so taken up in finding little extras for her chicks to eat, Mrs. Hen found herself and family charged into again. Leaping into the air, Mrs. Hen came down with wings flapping, ready for a fight, but Mr. Mongoose was gone. Crying chicks were scattered everywhere. In her own state of terror, Mrs. Hen collected her babies together behind her and again hurried away from the spot of attack.

Her chickens were under her, comforted between her feathers. But Mrs. Hen clucked anxiously, knowing she'd lost another chick. Yet worse was to happen.

In all, for six days, every day, Mr. Mongoose

strolled into the yard and carried off and ate one of Mrs. Hen's chickens.

On that awful final morning when her last baby had been carried off, Mrs. Hen was thrown into a kind of madness. Her hurt was more than a terrible sadness, for herself and for the pain of her lost chicks. Her loneliness was strange and peculiar. Without her chickens, the last one gone, it was as if she couldn't see, feel, or hear anything and didn't know how to be herself. She found herself going about the yard, clucking, calling. Then she found herself searching for her old nest. Mrs. Hen came to it and stood over it, looking in. She stepped into the old nest and sat down. Empty of eggs, empty of chicks, the nest was peculiar. It offered no peace, no comfort. All silly and miserable, Mrs. Hen gave up the sitting and walked about the yard, clucking, calling, wishing for a miracle that'd make her chickens appear.

A voice came from nowhere. "So you're like me now," it said.

Mrs. Hen looked up and saw Mrs. Ground Dove on a low tree branch. "Yes," she replied. "I'm like you now. My whole family! My whole family! My whole family! I've lost my whole, whole family. . . . What can I do? What can I do?"

"You could take that beast Mr. Mongoose to court," Mrs. Ground Dove said. "You could take him to court."

Mrs. Hen looked away in great, great surprise and wonder. She'd never thought of taking Mr. Mongoose to court. "Yes," she whispered. "Yes! That *is* something I can do. That really *is* something."

"It is, isn't it?" Mrs. Ground Dove said. "I'll watch for the outcome. Good luck."

Mrs. Hen took Mr. Mongoose to court.

Mr. Mongoose was escorted by a policeman into court. Mrs. Hen's charges against him were to do with attack, robbery, and murder of her six baby chicks.

Mrs. Hen sat waiting for the trial to begin.

She was all excited inside. She wanted to make sure she told what happened clearly and properly. She was getting everything orderly and clear in her head when something struck her. Mrs. Hen noticed that every policeman in the court was a Mr. Mongoose. The clerk of the courts was a Mr. Mongoose. The prosecutor was a Mr. Mongoose. And the judge—the judge who'd just come in and sat down—was an older and big-bellied Mr. Mongoose. Every official who ran the court was a Mr. Mongoose! Mrs. Hen was shocked, horrified, panic-stricken. She'd never felt more ganged up against, more exposed, more tricked! Mrs. Hen's shock and worry turned into a tight pain across her tummy. Mrs. Hen wanted to talk to somebody official. She wanted to talk to somebody!

Mrs. Hen pulled herself together, telling herself not to be silly. This was a court of law. It didn't matter who the officials were. It didn't matter one bit who the officials were.

Then, as if everything happened far, far

away, Mrs. Hen heard the officials of the court using her name a lot. The court was actually in session. Her case had started.

At last it was Mrs. Hen's turn to tell her case against Mr. Mongoose. She told the court how Mr. Mongoose attacked her and her family and robbed her of all her baby chicks. Every day for six days Mr. Mongoose attacked her and her family and robbed her of all her baby chickens. He took all of the six she had. That same Mr. Mongoose standing there in court robbed her badly, brutally, and murdered her babies. And not one was left with her. Not one. And she was heartbroken and sad. She was asking the court to make Mr. Mongoose repay her for the loss of her family, for their suffering, and for her suffering. And she was asking the court to punish Mr. Mongoose. And to stop him from making any such attack on her or anyone else ever, ever again.

The court listened to Mrs. Hen patiently. The court listened to her until she was completely finished.

Then one Mr. Mongoose court official in a gown got up and spoke. And oh, the Mr. Mongoose court official in his gown broke up Mrs. Hen's story badly. He broke up her story and changed it badly, badly. And from then on every other Mr. Mongoose court official talked about only the broken-up and changed story. And the same Mr. Mongoose in the gown began to laugh, saying, "My good lady, Mrs. Hen, how can you actually bring a case like this to court against someone without proof? Without any proof whatsoever?"

"I hope you understand your case, Mrs. Hen," the Mr. Mongoose judge said. "You have no evidence. You have no witnesses to prove that what you accuse Mr. Mongoose of is true. You have no witnesses. Do you understand that?"

Mrs. Hen did not understand. But she didn't answer. She was too, too shocked and bewildered with disbelief at what she saw the judgment would be. And truly, Mrs. Hen lost her case.

Alone again, Mrs. Hen started walking home.

Mrs. Hen walked slowly across a field. Dazed, hardly able to move, she walked slowly on and on. Sad, sad—Mrs. Hen's loneliness made her feel she walked in deepest darkness in a tunnel underground. And she carried the weight of the world. Her body was weighed down, awkward, heavy. She could hardly walk. Really, it was her sadness that gripped her. Her sadness held her full of tears that would not come. Her head felt all aspin. And the same thoughts went around and around: "Cruelty . . . dishonesty and cruelty! . . . I'm lost . . . lost . . . . Mongooses have all the say. All the authority. It makes all mongooses say yes! yes! yes! It makes them feel strong being dishonest and cruel. Their strength's their cruelty and self-deceit—all wrapped, well wrapped, in a pretence that looks like shining respectability. . . . Cruelty crushed me. Oh—cruelty crushes you! . . . And I have no more words. . . . I'm lost . . . lost. . . ."

Unexpectedly, under a tree, a Mr. Mongoose stood in front of Mrs. Hen. Swiftly Mrs. Hen was surrounded by one, two, three, four Mr. Mongooses. Everything about them was menacing. Every move and look on their faces was set with violence, attack, death. As they were closing in, Mrs. Hen looked straight at one of the Mr. Mongooses. She whispered, "But today—you—you were my judges!"

All four Mr. Mongooses held Mrs. Hen. They gripped her tight and hard. They killed Mrs. Hen. And with noisy celebration, the four Mr. Mongooses ate Mrs. Hen.

ALSO BY JAMES BERRY

A Thief in the Village and Other Stories
Spiderman Anancy
When I Dance: Poems
Ajeemah and His Son